Add your Book Title here

Add your Author Name here

Published in 2017 by FeedARead.com Publishing

First Edition

A CIP catalogue record for this title is available from the British Library.

INTRODUCTION

This story begins with darkness and then it gets a little darker its basically a story about how Benjamin messing up not just at work but in his home and in his mind. It goes up and brings you back down with a bump. It is all about time and how it could destroys you mentally and physically. It is a journey from being appslutly happy to being totally sad and crazy. People say money cannot buy you happiness but I think the opposite for people that have never had a money it could be a good omen. In his case it is a good omen as Benjamin has lost his job through the things and the people that he keeps meeting. Taken into account who you do the things that Benjamin does if you had lost your job. The story takes a twist as he is left a bribe. It's a story of survival and guts.

PREFACE

Benjamin is a quiet and normal he is the main character which I want you to focus on has a little bit he could have been a police man. I gave him quite a few problems he was clever enough to figure it out. I wanted him to be a loner. Even though he had chance to mix with people mostly his wok mates I wanted him to be a loner. It was his show and I wanted it to be totally about him. This book is totally non-fiction and it take so you on a ride I think that the country side was the perfect place to start the book with the opening page setting the scene on the road in the night time. hard. I wanted him to be a postman.

CHAPTER ONE
THE PASSENGER

It was late I had just finished my night shift I was actually happy for once if you knew the things that I knew and had to deal with them you would be too. I had been watching parcels all morning and all day long the only satisfaction of the job, any job was that the fact that you would be helping somebody and of course the money, I was helping somebody somewhere out there. I was just finishing my work shift I could not tell you completely was going on, but deep down inside I knew that the company had a problem a big problem. We had everything you name it, it came through the post. And as we had it we were going to deliver it at a cost, it was the game. It all started in the winter I was under a lot of pressure. It began when I received a parcel I did not have any idea what was in it but it did not seem right it did not seem like a normal parcel. I could have sent it back to the parcel office but somehow, I manage to convince myself that I should keep it. As for bottle goes I was scared most of the day not knowing what I was delivering, I was paranoid, parcel after parcel I would deliver. Not knowing what I was delivering. I heard through the grape vine the word on the street was taking over making our jobs even harder it was now a game. I had to think about that even though I was practical and it probably had nothing to do with me even though I was concerned. I was standing in the parcel room thinking what was I doing as another parcel dropped of the conveyer belt in to the postal sack. Once I had my load I was ready, jumped into my van, I was looking for a smoke as it was the only time that I could smoke other than on the streets as I leant over the hot black leather seats into my glove compartment for my smokes I eventually found them I pulled the packet open with my teeth and quickly pushed the stereo on with the other hand at the same time leaving the vercel unmanned, it was dangerous. Well it was dangerous anyway in fact anyway I was thinking that it had not been a day that I had not picked a fight this year or caused somebody in the office grief it was not easy being a postman you would understand if you were one. I mean the kind of places that you had go the worse places where the slums backed together with pizza delivery leaflets not just a few but hundreds what was the point of that if I wanted a pizza I would go to the local kabab they have always got it on the menu or even more so a restaurant. Second the dodgy parcel probably filled with dope. All I am being a post man, they get there shit through me I do not like that. Day in and day out the same roads the same doors some of our customers are quite nice mind you it is not all bad some of our customers are quite actually thank us some of our customers thank us by the door. It is always good to meet people in doorways and if you're lucky you might even get a smile that's what it's about that kind of attitude could make you and break you. I was in the category of being happy and broken.

At this point my day was just finishing and I was on my way back to the post office I was telling myself that it had not been a bad day. But just as those thoughts left my car hit something on the road I presumed that it was road kill as I hit it I served of the road losing control of my van, the van then steered its self as I had lost control. I hit some road side bushes and ended up off the road after smashing down on the steering wheel and hitting the horn of the car in total frustration. I got out of the car and checked it for ant damage. There was minor damage nothing serious, a flat tire. I was looking back down the road I must have hit a rock somewhere back there. Before I got back into the verse I had to know what I had hit I took the cars keys out of the ignition and locked the van, heading around the back of the van I opened the back doors as I did I thought I heard something but I ignored it as I moved the parcel around looking for the torch, it was a pen torch you would think that the company would have supplied me with something a little more heavy duty. I slammed the boot door shut with the torch pen in my mouth. And on I went down the lane to see what I had hit. I had walked around forty yards when I had found him a young man about twenty may be twenty-four I stopped thinking and went into shock I could not find the words to say anything it just laid there I was standing up absorbing it all in. Then there was a reaction. My face became hot and just as I realized that I had run somebody down which I thought was road kill just began to tear me apart. I was just standing over him looking at his face it was still. I was pacing around thinking farcically how I was going to explain this to the police or my boss it was not good that I was in the country side with no witnesses and not in town. I was thinking least nobody saw it, but that did not help. As I was pulling myself together I was going through his jacket pockets he had no id. For some reason and it seemed strange and it had to be a coincidence that there would be none. As I became more panicky I remembered not to move the body. When I shone my torch down into the bushes to see what he had lost I found a parcel. I was lucky I could have disregarded it as country side rubbish. On it had some words I just looked down on them not taking them into my mind all I knew at that point was it was or could be a clue to what was in the package. There was a no address on the parcel and I could not open it at it was illegal so by not being able to know what it was it went straight to the back of the van. It was named as undelivered and went to the back of the van with the rest of the undelivered parcels.

I left the body where I had found it and I called the authority's, I was telling myself that it was the right thing to do but I was also telling myself that this might not be good. All in all, it took them about twenty minutes to arrive just enough time to think my story through. And of course, I had to explain everything to them. eventually it took me eight and a half hours to convince them and even then, they were not ready to let me go I was straight, and not under any influences they finally let me go. When I got out of the police station I went back to the van I took all the parcels and walked home. as my van was now part of the evidence. I also had to explain to my boss. I was not a happy bunny and he was not happy about the company van. I did not think that it was my fault all he did is give me another set of keys to another van and told me to get back to work. I asked my boss if I should start straight away he was kind enough to send me home until the afternoon. When I got him I just dumped the bag of envelopes and parcels in my hall way floor I only had a few hours and I wanted to sleep. I was looking out of the window thinking how beautiful the skies were and kind of getting sentimental about old things, mostly the past and what had happened in the last couple of days. I tried to sleep but all I could think about was what had happened the last couple of days, the accident was all I could see. the visions would never will never go away. I thought that that was good but however it was bad I could not get the picture of the boy out of my mind. I did not get the right amount of sleep there was no way that I was going back to work today. Eventually time set in. and I knew that I could get away with it, it was a perfect excuse for taking the day off. And that's as it was. I laid there for a few hours with a blanket the worst part of it was the waking up and even more so being awake and trying to sleep even so. I stayed put I stayed in bed, and I was explained by my boss that the next time we were to meet would be in his office.

Eventually I fell asleep and it was the roughest night that I had ever had. As I awoke it was like being pinned down it was like sleeping with my eyes open half conscious.

CHAPTER 2
THE HARD DRINK

After the last day's occurrences, I needed a drink I was trying so hard to get the image of the dead boy out of my mind and I had to admit it was not going to be easy it was like having a dead relative the tears and thought s never leave you. I had just woken up so I needed a wash, I stripped down out of my clothes and went into the bath room after folding my clothes in to a pile leaving them on the end of my bed the whole thing about the boy echoed through my mind the hot water ran smoothly down my back taking the thoughts away although I could of stayed in the water for ever but in the end I knew that I would have eventually have to give up and walk away. I left the shower and dried myself off on the way out. I laid on my bed leaving the towel on the floor to dry. It was going to be a good day and with that I was pulling another sicky which mint I had another couple of days off. I laid there on my bed not wanting to move, not wanting to see the day light, not wanting to speak and not wanting to eat or at that moment at that point wanting to drink. The confusion felt incredible as the images of the boy was slowly subsiding I was feeling a little better about myself.

Except there was a strange feeling in my room almost like a present almost ghost like it was the air the way it moved around my mind. It was really weird it was like nothing, but something. I had no choice but to go back to sleep as I slept I began to dream. I was dreaming of the boy that I found dead in the country side lane again in this dream he was standing in front of me. I was in the van and he was standing on the middle of the road he was speaking I could not hear what he was saying I woke up as I was just about to read the words off his mouth. As you cannot speak in dreams, in this dream, although in the rest of the dream I was in the van and the boy in front of me and as dreams only last around three minutes and are usually in the morning. I disregarded it as a nightmare.

Although after thinking about it a lot I wanted to know if it meant anything, I needed a schizophrenic a medium, to tell what the dream meant. It was not going to be easy as I could not just pick up the phone book and call one. In the end, I, had lost I think I thought about the idea to much and was blowing this out of proportion. I and was not keen on walking around town looking for one. And then I just thought I could just drown my sorrows so I did now to my surprise it was quite a little different. As I remember I was at the store I did not like walking into places that I never really go too. I did not like drawing attention to myself. As I walked through the isle, looking at everything and at the end finding the beer. I paid for them at the counter I had grabbed a few cans of beer. The lady at the counter was polite and nice although I was a loner and I was not keen on making new friends not because I did not have any it was the other way around I had too many, I preferred to keep myself to myself however she was pretty.

I paid the lady her money and stepped out the shop my mind racing. It was nice to be in the warm air filling my body it was nice to be warm. As I opened the first can. By mid-day I was drunk and home. I clambered to my front door it was my neighbours lucky they were not in I had stood there for about five-minute playing with my keys and his lock it took me around ten minutes all in all just to figure that one out.

This time I was on the wrong floor being in mind that I was drunk all the doors where the same at that point in my mind. And that does not say a lot for me as I am a postman. When I finally found the right door, which was mine I walked in throwing the keys on to the table but missing completely and losing them somewhere on my floor. I decided to sit down. I did not want to be sober, as I sat down on my chair slowly counting the thoughts. As I opened another beer telling myself that it would be okay it was just a drink, but it was not.

As the day went on I was getting more and more upset at the fact that I had run somebody down and I could not get the image out of my mind I turned to the bottle again and again but only for a few days I was knocking them back. At this point as I put the glass down and imagine d what would be left of my imagination of what I was going though., as the authorities had already questioned me I believed that I was going to be cleared at this point I had already forgotten about the parcel my thoughts where elsewhere obliviously. As the day went on I was passing in and out of consciousness thinking about one thing and then another what was the passenger and why was it written on the dead boy's parcel. I hung my head down thinking that I had could not find an answer. Half drunk and and drooling out of the side of my mouth. I had nearly run out of beer the only hang hat was keeping me sane. I was on the verge of passing out the images the dead boy would not move an inch. It was beginning to frighten me. I wanted to go back to the scene the place that I had found him I was concerned about him where he would stand spiritually and if I could help. As I began to think I began to dream of him the word s passenger kept on recurring through my sleep I would wake up saying the word to myself although I did not know what it meant if anything at all. I was all over the place I was about to pass out again for the second time. This was happening in my home. as the beer wore itself in I began to laugh one minute I was laughing the next I was minute I was screaming and the next shouting. I was finding it too easy to find these emotions it was real. Although anybody who was anybody would have probably said I was crazy I had lost it in modern terms. I really had to think about the situation that I was falling into. I was not happy. All I wanted to do was to think and drink, I could have put a hundred reasons why but with the mind I could just blank it out. The clouds and the sky moved on wards the night came quickly. I was minding my own business as the sun went down sending darkness upon everything as I hit another bottle trying to think and ignore that I had killed some kid a teenager and I think that I had a good reason to hit the bottle. I was walking around in a drunken state as I was now using the bottle for an excuse it was not like me as I slowly sobered up I was quick to start it up all over again and I was happy but it left me in the wrong state of mind. I wanted mine to be heaven it looked like I was going to hell. Going all the way back I finally convinced myself that it was not fault. I was driving home I did not see the victim I kept telling myself over and over.

In the end, I was going to see the police again with ant accident or murder there was going to be a trail. I had a phone call I was scared I wanted to get out and get out fast the courts gave me a day to gather my story I had no choice but the day came to the trail I was not worried as the day before. The court room was filled with people most of them I did not recognize I did not trust ant of them I was in the dock. The questioning began question after question after question. To the point that I was getting ear ache less alone a heart attack, they were slowly breaking me down yet I had done nothing wrong. All I needed was a drink to calm me down after being cross examined twenty times I was still in the dock slowly losing my mind. Until it came to the point that I told them the truth from the start and to the end to the tee, no lies. I explained it as it was as it happened I was waiting for the verdict. I asked the judge if I could leave the dock after about five minutes if that I was asked to re-enter the darkness of the room was sending my mind way back. Question after question. What if I had driven the other way around. I explained, I answered all the questions in the defence of myself. This accident was not my fault I was not speeding which the court presumed, I was not under any pharmaceutical's or under any other kind of drugs which include marurina, amphetamine which is speed, whiz, LSD or cocaine. They gave the verdict not guilty. When I left the dock, I was angry but happy. I walked down through the court room with the permission too as I left the court rooms. That's when I woke upside down and in my bed drooling. I reached out just about conscious and managed to grab a towel which in the end was a sock and wiped the saliva from my mouth. In dis taste realizing what I was doing through the sock back onto my floor. I rolled on to my bed onto I fell on to the floor and staying there until I could get off the floor half awake and sober, I needed a cigarette I got up feeling happy but not happy enough to dye I threw my jeans and went out for a smoke. As I was slowly pulling the smokes out of my suit jacket pocket and putting a smoke into my mouth I laid on my bed for a moment before going outside. Then I lit it the smooth sensation hit my throat. As it passed through my air ways into my system I was now feeling relaxed. And the thought of the boy had dispersed for now.

CHAPTER 3
HARD TIMES

When I looked back into my past I was a reasonable poor kind of chap as a child, I had not the kind of things that my closest friend shad. And I spent a lot of time of thinking why. I wanted the same things as them but never really thought of it. I wanted to work and to work hard for it but being so young I never got the opportunity that were placed in front of me because I could not see them for being so young. Although I was unhappy threw this I just wanted to be like any other kid on the street it was not going to happen just yet so I had to put up with the bullying and the second-hand comments from other teenagers I suppose you could call it per pressure something which has grown with as I have grown up. In the end the street was going to get me and I was going to get the street.

I was all absorbing it in, everything I had the notion that I should watch everything and everyone. I would question my friends on a day to day basis and people that I would meet just on passing ion the street. I did not wake up but I did grab myself another a beer opening it up drinking it straight down my eyes on the ceiling. As I took another sip as I looked around the celling wishing that I could be somewhere else. Not forgetting the time as I would have to be back at work soon. I closed my eyes again thinking of the body I was beginning to think that I had killed somebody. I did not bump over him I would have felt it in the vans chassis the feeling of knowing that you may have killed someone was incredible not to my taste though I was getting really upset. In the morning, I, had sobered up and I had decided to go back to the scene for some stupid reason, I needed to know the truth. When I had got there all I could see was tape the road had been closed off. I had a can of beer with me, good. I had something to keep me calm I opened it on entering the scene. I approached the site slipping under the tape and looked onwards at the white shape that the body had left.

I had nothing I wanted to believe that I had hit a deer, it was not to be. I could have bet a bunch of twenty's that I was setting myself up. I finally agreed that I was wrong and I was right that I hit him. But there were many questions like what was he doing walking in the country side at that hour with no torch? The point though now was that I had run him over. I needed therapy I was going mad. I made my way back to the car and got in putting the keys into the ignition and turning the engine on I wanted to drive back home but instead I sat there in the car just gripping the stirring wheel. Even though I had been cleared I still felt like I was going down. I did not want to tell anybody I was feeling guilty. I paid my respects and drove off in to the distance back home forgetting what was in the parcel in the back of the van. I was alone as the smooth wind blew around me it was if it ws following me. I went back inside to grab another beer force of habit now that I had met it. the echoes of my mind echoed through me as I opened another bottle of beer the body was on my mind it was like the slow blowing of the air with several things it was teasing me like the devil. I closed my eyes. The music in the background and everything was perfect. But it was not I pulled another smoke out of the packet and lit it up I felt like scrooge but the other way around. The lights from the road side a neighbour's lights hit my house it was enlightening but it made no difference. I pulled hard on what was left of the cigarette that I was smoking and felt around in my jacket for another. All that I could find was a packet of papers I had run out of smokes.

I thought of the body again as I was at home I had the opportunity of going down fridge for another beer I seemed to be hitting the beer a lot lately but that was only to block out the accident it was not working. It eased my mind from all the fright and the thoughts, even though there was a chance that I could have missed him. But I hit him and he was dead. I really wanted to tell myself that I hit a deer but that would be very lucky.

The van was at the depot so I could not see the excite damage I should have checked it out properly. As I looked out of my study window I kind of thought I was thinking that the whole thing was a dream I wanted it to be a dream. I was sure when I reached the body that it was already dead. I went through this scenario over and over. I should have checked the body and it was just coincidence that I just happened to stop. Although on top of that I took the parcel. It did not make me feel any better. I laid in bed thinking that I was having a hard time so what it could have happened to anybody, I laid there further maybe it did not. Maybe it was just that I had run out of luck. I did not know I closed my eyes and pulled my pillow closer to me and began to think how I could get myself out of this mess. It was true I was screwed just as the next person if it had happened to me it would have probably happened to someone else I closed my eyes thinking why me. what have I done the remorse was really kicking in. thinking deeply there had to be a solution. I was going all the way back to the start. But it made no difference, as far as I could look. Back into my mind nothing changed in my stories or in my vision even in my dreams. Everything was the same. The body and the parcel.

CHAPTER 4
THE GIRL

In every story, there must be a girl in my case she was the ugliest and most horrible looking that man and god could have sent to me. it was now obvious that god had clearly got it in for me both ways. When I looked at her I could not even think and I could not even think of having sex, although every time she approached in the office she had that look in her eyes. Her name I cannot recall right now but she was a big one I do not mean that to sound persist hence the comment. Even though that she was a big girl she was well bubbly the big girls always are, and it was obvious to me that her and myself were gagging for it.

As I was new to the office as I had only been working here for around half a year that would be six months I was getting to know the office that I was working in she was always there to correct my mistakes. It was weird that I did not notice her help before. It was also embarrassing but I had to except her help as a colleague every time she approached me a big smile came up upon my face she would ask me what was so funny and I would answer nothing and continue my work. It was obvious that there would be a possibility that I was going to end up with her if you know what I mean. As much as I was trying to avoid it.

When she approached me on this occasion she managed to push me in to a position with one arm out blocking me and the entrance what would have been my exit route. She started with a chat up line it did not impress me she knew by the look on my face. she hit me another that s when I saw the badge she was the manage. I was standing with one hand leaning on the desk besides me. she continued you know the drill the drill I said, you know if you want that promotion, promotion I replied. Then I told her straight well that was not me I was saying I was happy I continued although the extra money would be good however I do not want to sleep with you. She continued for a while but was slowly giving in. The pressure in the room was getting to much. For the rest of the day every she was calling upon me do this do that get this get that. Calling me back again and again complaining that my work was not right sending me back to the start to do it all over again. I could her words echoing through my thoughts if you do not shag me I will send you to the end. The end I thought what did she mean then well I will tell you mail boy handling the rest of the boys pays checks I had known idea what she meant.

I was getting nervous as she was continually approaching me day after day, I was beginning to get the picture she shags me all over her. She would get close to me close enough to whisper in my ear she was the way up. I could not believe it what I was hearing If I was to deny her any further it would probably lose my job. She approached me again. This time she was strong but I knew that it was just an act. A typical fat girl act. I was slowly bowing down to her and knew that she was extremely persistent.

This time she went to kiss me I knew that was going to happen and it still took me by surprise. As she planted her lips upon me I stood there I was going into shock. Her lips were glued to me it was like I was being eaten, as she clung on them with her hands around my bottom and her face squashed into mine I was trying to pull myself away as I did she clung on even harder I finally pushed her off and she walked off. Then with no because she called out for me to follow her I was a little reluctant as I knew that she was asking me for sex. Not that I minded except I did not want to do it with her. Mind you it could be away to a promotion it was the way up into a better job. I would be crazy not to except her invitation although I still had to think about it. I could feel the echoes of her thoughts entering my head telling me to follow her. I could only imagine where she was leading me too. In the end, I decided to stay put mind you it was not like me to not do as I was told I did not move. I got back to work instead. I was counting the packages and envelopes, at the end of the day I went home. when I got inside I went straight for an ice-cold beer which was unusual for me. I was not a drinker but on this occasion I thought that I deserved it, as I had a strange day at work. As I laid on my bed half awake and half sober I found myself to be in an irritable mood with nothing to watch on TV.

I was skipping through the channels finding it hard to find something that was normal to watch. I closed my eyes and thought about the thoughts of the day. I was trying hard not to think about my boss. But then on the other hand it might be a good thing. I was thinking no more cooking and no more cleaning and no more company sex. I took another mouth full of beer it was great so far. When I opened my eyes after a few minutes I felt a little bit better but that was not the cure. I did not know why I was thinking about that girl the manager. Even though I was straight the thought seemed to fit but I was not right if you know what I mean. I was gathering my thought and pulling them into me. thinking that as much as I liked her as she was my boss I was not into fat girls. No offence.

CHAPTER 5
THE MOVE

I was sitting in my chair by my window staring out into the darkness. It was something which I had always loved the night. Properly more than the day light. As I sat there by the window I did not know that something was ticking away., the package. Even though I was in a safe place and knew that I was at home there was a new feeling and I could feel that something had changed. The atmosphere did not seem right. In fact, my home did not feel lie my home. As this feeling became more and more uncomfortable. I had decided that it was probably my imagination and I should spend more time outside. Rather than inside my home at that time was little short of a mansion it was situated by a lake. Even though we were half way through winter I told myself to try and spend some time by the becalming lake which was basically my back garden. I was now sitting outside on my balcony with my eyes closed I was not meditating as such however the images that I could see where not as I wanted to perceive. I was not on anything which include street drugs or medication and my condition excited me.

So, the question was where being these images coming from and what did they mean. I was struggling to keep up with it and I found it addictive. I was too scared to tell my doctor and I was too scared to tell anybody that the fact was I could see. even though I knew that it was not normal. And I did not even think for a minute it was or could be normal. Because I was normal and only a normal guy would agree. As I was sitting outside by the lake it became my escape back to reality it was like I was running away from god. I wanted to tell my friends but every time I found the right time I would bottle it all up. Every time I approached them I would become a bumbling mess. I would stutter and in the end I would just turn the conversation around back into something normal in the end. Time was flying by it was coming to close of winter I would always find myself on the lake it was a beautiful day, I would sit there day after day and week after week month after month watching the images that were in me. Trying to understand what I was visualizing I could everything and other times nothing. I was not a scientist I was a postman. I was not totally mad yet and the dreams and visions that I was having where not of a normal man and I was beginning to believe that they had spiritual meaning and I needed someone to explain them to me like a medium.

To start off with the visions seemed normal but as time went on they became more and more frequent and I became more and more distant. Eventually I could not see them clearly. The only thought was to write them down. I would wake up in the morning if you could call it waking up and find myself in the toilet with the sink taps running how I got there I did not know properly there was a possible chance that I had been sleep walking. I was not feeling sick but needed to relieve myself. I was pursuing my thought s as the echo of the water ran down and rang through my mind it did not seem normal anymore. I jumped my eyes where that sensitive and I reach out for a towel to hind them from the light I had missed what I was trying to grab and fell to the bathroom floor. Probably low blood pressure. I do not know the real reason that was only a guess. I could recall feeling dizzy at the time. I was lucky not to have fallen on to the sick and caused myself some real damage.

When I finally awoke, I checked myself over, good there was nothing broken and no bruises.

It was now early evening and I was getting ready for a night shift. I already knew that I was going to be late and I knew that the boss was going to grill me. it was funny as I walked through my home there seemed to be a present at first I disregarded it as a vision, a ghost perhaps, it was clear white and I could see its hair it looked brown and it looked like the boy. I stopped and thought of talking to it. I wanted to question it I wanted to know if it could talk. They were my thoughts at that moment however at this point I did not approach it as I did not know the outcome. It was very spooky and it made me feel a little bit out of place. It was just hovering in front of me. and before I had a chance to think about it was in front of me. I had started to think about it I thought I heard it speak I was not sure. As much as it was

intriguing that I had might have met a phenomenon I had to get to work.
When I got to work, I was greeted and I was on a high until I had met my boss who was not particular happy about me being two hours late, I was in his office trying to explain. He brought me down quickly. It was not nice and he was not nice. In the end after a long conversation he sent me home with a big warning. When I got home, I had calmed right down as I spent most of the journey home swearing. I was greeted almost straight away by this spiritual being or ghost I was sure which one it was. It started to speak with me and I started to talk to it. I close to question it and it seemed happy enough to me to ask it questions it was almost dream like. The question I asked it was, was I in danger and the second was how much in danger was I. I was asking it hard questions but he seemed to make no sense in what I saying and did not answer me. I then asked him if he had an age he said twenty I did not catch on at first then I clicked and realized that it was the boy. I started to feel a little bit out of place after that he said he had to go but I had one more question just as he started to disappear I asked him if I would see him again there was no answer he departed. I really hoped that was the end of it.

CHAPTER 6
BIRTHDAY BOY

It was my birthday however I was on my own again and to top it off I did not get a text message phone call from anybody. Although I knew what little family I had they were thinking about me. even though I had not seen any of my relative for years and years. The thought was a little bit interesting. After two or three beers, the tears began to flood in and the day had begun. I was choking up in a big way, and the music was there too. Some romantic song just brought it all back. I quickly found myself a smoke and the tears continued uncontrollably down my face. I was concerned about myself. I had beaten myself up. My emotions had stirred themselves up and I was getting more and more upset. As I wiped the tears from my face and pushed the tears from my eyes old memories began to take over leaving me the wrong state of mind I was feeling rather cool. But I was still upset. As the day, past I continued to drink until I was totally drunk. It was a habit that I was not used to, but slowly getting used too. In my mind, I was thinking that it was my birthday so I was pleased that I could break the rules. The evening had come slowly and I had the chance to sit outside in the moonlight. On this occasion, there was a full moon. I thought about that a lot, the stars in the sky and the wind in the trees about me with the soft blowing breeze. As the wind blew into my face it was cooling me down and sobering me up preparing me for the next larger. As I smiled as it was so soothing I stayed there all night. There was not much else I could do to cheer myself up now. It was not even that late in the evening and I was drunk and wanted to get even more drunk. As I walked around in fact I was in tears thinking about what I was experiencing I was lost for words. There was not much that would cheer me up now. Everything seemed to be right but when I closed my eyes inside my soul was telling me something different. The next question was what I did not understand it and I had no one to talk too. So, I had to explain it to myself the only thought was to talk to my doctor and I already knew what he was going to say it was more likely that he would something along the lines of shove a load of pills down myself a top myself in his terms but they were nice and just said take some medication. You know that really helped, I did not. It was a dirty system. I decided to avoid them as much as possible. It was funny that

I had come to that conclusion as I had heard of it before. As I was drunk it gave me the excuse to think about these things. I thought the thought would surpass, well I hoped it would, it did not I was left thinking about some weird things I had also began to worry. I looked down into it as the day went on and I was sure that it was a warning like most things that I get into or think about. I was totally drunk sitting on and outside on my balcony. Something was stirring I was right I had the over whelming feeling that I was being watched even more so I could feel that something was not right. This feeling I had I had felt this feeling before. It was the same feeling that I had experience when I first found the body. This so-called feeling was beginning to bother me I had the feeling was not right all day long. In fact, all week long. What I was supposed to be looking for I did not know just yet. Was it an item or something that I had writ down. As I looked out of my window standing there looking out wards across the lake I was thinking that it was my birthday still. I pulled my phone from my pocket to see if I had any messages I had none, it did not surprise me as I had just moved into the area and since I had been busy settling down I did not have the chance to give out my address or telephone number. I never really got to tell my friends my contact number and looking at it realistically they properly were not my friend s in the first place horrible as it may seem but that s is just the way it is that is just life. After thinking about it, it brought tears to my eyes it was the Past. I was getting upset again and the tears began to rise although I knew it was probably the drink. It was getting late now, I had been outside now for quite a while on the balcony, I was slowly watching the day turn to night it was almost dream like. It took a couple of minutes for the clouds to disappear and the night to fall.

I stood outside for a few more moments I agreed that it was quite a special place as I Had walked into my house again the feeling of uncertainly and danger became my thought. I should have listened to it but at that point I did not believe it. I was brought up differently to that. I looked outside again my doors were open now the cold air blew in until I shut the door it was getting late.

I was waiting for a letter from my boss or even a phone message to invite me back to work I did not think that he would fire me I did not think he had the bottle. even so I checked my e-mails and phone messages there was nothing. I guessed that it was the way it was. I guess he was not the family man that he perceived himself as. It did not hurt too much. I closed my eyes and wished myself a happy birthday even so now I continued to celebrate, into the early hours of the morning.

I was playing music to the early hours of the morning. Playing music extremely loud, it was fun I was kind of happy. I was dancing around the house. And as it only happens once a year I could do it again. When the morning arose, I found myself laying on my floor I was clinching an opened bottle of beer and my only words where err. I must have passed out. The music was still on except the record was skipping so I had woken up to a half-eaten bag of crisps which were everywhere there was other food there as well one half eaten kabab which I was sure that I did not order but was there any way. This was weird as I could not even remember that I had ordered it. Any way what was done was done I could not change the past. After a couple of cigarettes, I began to come down and I was slowly sobering up. It was time to clear up. There were cans all over the place and I was surprised that I had drank so much. I was finding things like party poppers and other weird things. I turned the record off which was continually skipping. I turned the volume up as I was looking around the room I came across more beer cans and glasses more and more beer cans in could not believe that I had drunk so much either way the feeling was good it felt destructive even though I had not damaged anything or anyone.

Just as I was finishing the room I was well and I thought that it was another birthday over for another year. I had put what remained into a dustbin bag and and took the mews to the front of the house. It was chile and dark. That party was over.

CHAPTER 7
THE SYNDICATE

THERE WAS SOMETHING THAT I DID NOT KNOW THAT THE POST OFFICE WAS A SYNDICATE.

It was full of criminals, what their crime was, well I will tell you they were bringing it in. To be honest it was not something that I would care to discuss or even talk about however on this occasion I would like to enlighten your mind and talk about it. Going all the way back when I first got my job. Which explains why everybody was so friendly and why the boss was trying to lay me, I had been watching the factory for ages. I mean to say it was so obvious to me a partly whiskered cat could have smelled it, but they did not care and the only thought was the money. It was not like me to think about this but they were on my mind, as I watched every parcel come in and go out there was seven and the seven workers that were bringing it in. How did it work I do not know exactly, but what I did know that it was there I wanted some evidence on what I was believing and what I was seeing? I went out to my van and I had a camera on, but by phone. It was not that bad of a van knowing now that it could bring it in. I opened the door and leant inside. How did it work I do not know exactly, but what I did know that there needed to be evidence on what I was seeing and believing? I went outside to my van it was not that bad of a verse I mean who would think that a post van would bring it in. I opened the door and leant inside, pushing the parcels aside reaching for my phone in my glove compartment and as it was a guess that it would be there found it. I shut the van door watching and making sure that there was nobody around me. I was thinking that I had uncovered one extremely large scam.

I locked the van door and went up back to the office, I was excited I started filming everything. The work team did not seem to care as they were out of it in normal terms that was getting high. That's what I was thinking. Except when I approached one of my work mates he was not particularly nice. That gave it away and gave me an eye opener. I was trying to tell him that I was making a film for my daughter which was the excuse for bring the camera to work and that's why bi was doing the filming. Even though I did not have a daughter. As I gathered the evidence he came after me, first grabbing my shoulder then pushing me he was clearly out of it he really lost his temper that's when I realized that it was not a good discussion to film here which gave me the notion that it was if you get the drift. It was oblivious hat the seven workers that I wanted to film, the syndicate knew what I was doing with the camera. It was not long before I had given myself away. I ended up in a small shuffle and had my phone taken lucky enough I managed to hold onto the camera. After they had approached me I did not bow down to the argument until the shuffle was noticed.

And I had an audience. As most of the office had stopped I tried to tell them it was just for publicity, but they were still persistent I was telling them to calm down. And I would erase the film. They continued still and insisted that I should hand over the camera. I told them it would not happen and called out to the rest of the workers for support. The argument was now over there was nothing that they could do. And they were told that they should go back to work or go home. In the end, they did and justice was done on this occasion. I kept on filming, I was in luck the postmen had turned away. I continued until I had met another girl, this time it was not the manager thank god. She had a lot of questions to ask me first she asked me if I

was okay I replied yes, I was fine then she asked me again and I replied the same she gave me an escape route by telling me that she would like me to film her I played along. She asked me what I was going to do with the film once it was finished I told her politely that I would probably stick onto the enter net. She did not by it and she knew that I was lying I could tell by the expression on her face but I had to try. What she did not know was that I was going study it. I managed to get my phone back most of the film that I had done with that was erased I put the phone in my pocket and continued my work, I was sorting out parcels now and I knew that I was behind the Schule, I finally got all my mail to deliver and left the office to go to go do the delivery.

I knew that I was going to the seven at some time as I was re-introduced by the the team manger she was a bitch and I knew that they knew what they were doing. The governor that was in charge was Jacob, he re-introduced me to some guy called matt who introduced me to some guy called mark who introduced me to mark who introduced me to Millie and it went on and on. I had made some so-called friends. I was not happy about this I was trying to hide the way I was feeling. From the expression of my face would tell it all I was trying to be careful not trying to get into something that I could not get out of. I was trying to hide away. To be honest being introduced to that many people in one day would make you kick off. As I looked around half amazed and half asleep due to the long day I was meeting more of them here's jams and Racheal and so. Honestly, I am impressed I said bowing down with my head over my shoulders. But in fact, it was the opposite deep down inside I was hoping to bring them down.

I continued my day but working with a company which was a drug cartel really upset me. I had to question myself and question my sanity that was all I could think about and hoped that my manger would contact me. he was probably in also. As the day went on the thought slowly aspired and I began to feel a little calmer all I wanted now was a beer. As soon as my hours were up I jumped into my van and headed into town looking for the nearest drink hole all I could find at that point was a petrol station but it was good enough I talked in it had that weird feeling even though I picked up some beers and a bottle of wine the wine was just for the sake of it. I paid the the man behind the counter the counter assistant and got back in to the van. Then being even more adventurious walked in to the nearest pub I walked out as it was not my style. There was no pressure on me now, I had my beer and that was enough for now. I went home.

CHAPTER 8
GOING BLIND

I was sitting in my van on my own it was not too late, as the traffic slowly disappeared and there was only a few cars on the road and went by. I slowly awoke as I had been asleep I could feel what was the remains of a hangover. And my only vice at that time was the noise of the traffic. It had not occurred to me that I had not opened my eyes yet. And I was blind but only for a moment, as soon as I realized my new problem I feel into shock. I was moving around the van. Shouting that I was blind. As I was moving around I was bumping my head which did not make the situation any better. I finally managed to get into the back seat. And with this shock and new occurrence past out. I knew where I was I knew the streets I was a postman. I was sure that you do not just go blind, so I was confident that my vision would return and come back. I laid in the back seat of the van. Lucky for me I was not just sitting there I was playing with a rube cube however I could not see the cube colours to see if I would win. I was still I was counting the turns and all the moves with the toy, I was coming up to the sixty fourth move and just stopped playing at that moment and I put the cube down. As I lent up to move into a more comfortable position leaning back hard against the car passage boor to get more comfortable. Just as I did there was a tap on the window and a voice. Who was it I asked then without an answer to my question I was questioned. It was excuse me sir you cannot park here. I was just trying to explain me knew situation. Then there was another voice she said the same as the other person who I believed was a male then I heard it again get out of the verse at point I was getting angry for being blind and for the traffic wardens were clearly not listening. I was trying to explain I was not particularly happy having to get out of the car, so I did not. I sat upright as I was previously laying back a little more than a gangster. As they approached the car they did not that I was blind I was telling them that I could not see. eventually I got out of the van and confronted them as I could only hear one voice I presumed that he was on his own I was mistaken there was two of them. As I got out of the car I felt weak my legs were about to buckle I collapsed onto both lucky they caught me putting them back onto my feet. At that point they did not know what the problem was. And it looked like I was trying to bundle them both over but that was not the case. As I tumbled over I brought both down I fell straight on top of both as I was apologising as I brought them to the ground. Through a lot of stinging nettles. I was in shorts which was normal and when the weeds stung they stung. After they had picked me up I quickly lost my balance again falling back into the side of the road and ended up in the same place in the stinging nettles bring them with this time. At this point, I was only wearing shorts and t-shirt falling into the bushes did not help. As I could not see my surroundings this time I was screaming in pain as I could feel my face swell up. And the pain in my arms and legs.

When we had all calmed down through this experience as I climbed out of the bushes my vision was slowly coming back. I could see a little better but not fully.

When I finally figured out where I was where I had parked my van. Again, I felt a shove on my shoulder it was a ticket as I could not see I went to speak to participant again I was denied. I stood there leaning back on the van, the thought was to rip the ticket up, I had an excuse I was half blind if the word got out to my boss I was sure that it would cost me my job. You can only make a certain number of mistakes. As I stood there a voice said to me that I did not want to do that. The two ticket wardens were still there watching me. I smiled and got back into the post van, slamming the door shut hurting myself even more. As I shuffled back into a more comfortable position and waited patiently for my vision to return to my eyes.

CHAPTER 9
LADY

I had just got home when I had seen her, she was a tramp the lady was pushing a shopping trolley she was wearing all black and wearing an old coat and it looked like she was carrying her wardrobe I stopped behind her taking what I was seeing all in to my mind. Now, I only had a couple of ten pound notes on me, I wanted to approach her in fact there was no way that I could have avoided her. She had settled right outside my home. I got out of my van locking it up securely. Then as I approached her as she was trying to fiddle around with something in her basket. I walked up to her thinking what had she done to become like that to be a second-class citizen on the streets I called out can I help you and what is your name she answered both of those questions at least she was thinking normal I guess that was lucky for me too. As I continued to speak to her our conversation became alive we had hit it off. I continued to question her until I felt that I could trust her to be invited in to my home. she seemed friendly enough so I did. I asked her into my home and she seemed delighted for the gesture although she had a big trolley and I asked her if she could leave it outside but she was extremely reluctant then I asked her what was in her trolley she replied her belongings. As I stood there thinking while she was thinking I decided to agree that she could bring the trolley into the house but she had to leave it by the front door. She has d answered all my questions.as we sat down for a cup of tea, she was grateful enough so I offered her something to eat her eye s light up with a smile a nod and a thank you.

We sat there for a few hours talking about how she got in to her position of being homeless and a lot about her past I was finding it exceptionally extraordinaire and completely compelling. I was upset for her at the end of the day she said that she should go and thank me for my hospitality. I thanked her in return for her company as I helped her with her trolley getting through the large front door. I wanted her to stay as she had nowhere else to go but as I did not really know her I let her leave. I was sure that I would see her again. I felt kind of guilty and hoped that she would be safe. As I thanked her for her company and helped getting her stuff through my front doors a back on to the street.

It was quite hard not to be able to think about the lady the tramp and I thought of not seeing her again, really broke my heart. I guess that that was just life in general. As the day went on I managed to put her aside and began to think of how I was going to go back to work. I was going to need a solid reason for the days that I had not turned up. I just know that I was going to get a blocking from the boss. I was thinking about what was going on in the depo. I was thinking about going back to work to do a late shift, I thought that I could get away with it but as it was already late evening I did not think that anybody would be there. As the day went on I could clearly see that the sun was setting and all I wanted to do was sleep. I had not felt this relaxed for a while I was feeling quite good I was telling myself that the meeting of the old girl had done something to me. so, it seemed, but it was probably my imagination, it came to the time to disregard her, horrible that it may seem.

I was upstairs sitting on the edge of my bed looking across the bed room while looking at my phone while looking at my chest of draws. I was expecting it to ring, as I had not been to work for a couple of days I was waiting for the boss to ring me and fire me. except she was probably high and properly had forgotten about me, which was good in a sense. If she had forgotten about me now it meant that I was still employed, she knew that she could not fire me as I knew the floor secrets as I climbed further back into my bed I closed my eyes.

I was now asleep but what seemed like ours was in fact only a few minutes I was tossing and turning all night long not exactly asleep. I would have called it half asleep or more to the point awake. And knowing that I had to be awake for five o'clock did not make things be any easier in the end I eventually gave up it was funny and weird I would morally just drop off. Without the right sleep, did not put me in the right mood I was sitting on the edge of my bed again mind you sitting there in silence seemed to stabilize my mood. The mood that I was in now was just made me close my eyes. As I did so I began to reminisce about the things of my past. The last few days' happenings. I wanted to blame somebody for the thing shat were happe3ning and the things that had happened. The parcel and the dead body.

The loss of my vison and the traffic wardens the problem at work and the tramp.

In the end, there was nothing to sum it all up. Nothing that I was trying to explain amounted to nothing. I was asking myself if I was cracking up. As the sun moved slowly across its sky. I could see it clearly from my bedroom window. I got off my bed and walked towards my curtains stretching out my arms pulled them open. It was bright outside with a little bit of dew and a large amount of mist. I turned away as I was undressed and went upstairs to find some clothes. I was walking through my hall way dressed with my head down and focussing on the day ahead of me. picking up my parcel bag on my way out. As I was now outside I locked the door and moved toward s the van, picking up my post bag that was laying in my door way opening the door and walking out into the fresh air.

As I was now outside I locked the front door and moved quickly to my van I opened the boot slamming down the bag of parcels into the boot and walked around to the driver's side to the door. as I opened the door I had a feeling that this was not going to be a good day. When I got into the driver's seat I took my keys out and slowly pushed them into the ignition. Locking all the doors and trapping myself inside. I was on my way to work again. As I drove to work the traffic was bad this did not help my situation I spent the best of an hour in traffic just hooting my horn, the rest of the time was moving extremely slow I do not know what I would call it. eventually the traffic got moving and I was on my way again it would probably surprise you that the amount of old granny's that I had to stop for would amaze you. I pulled up in the car park in the post office I was greeted by my boss I guess that I was out of luck I thought that I was going to be sent home again she did not approach me or say anything. That was kind of weird, she just stood there in the back ground. she was giving me a break not because I was being late but because she fancied me. I got back to work slowly the traffic had dispersed even so I had spent a good few hours in traffic and on my horn. Eventually the traffic began to move. I was on my way again it would surprise you how many grannies that there were trying to cross the street, it was an eye opener to me. I went straight to the main building and picked up my bag it had already been filled I took it back to the van, and off on my round to post the mail. I had still had some parcels from yesterday I knew that it was going to be a slay. As I drove down the road and the next road the same feeling that had occurred came over me.

I was walking again it felt good, the sun was beating down even though it was still winter. And there were people and cars I already knew the round over and I was grateful and the exercise it was great to be a postman.

CHAPTER 10
TWO DEAD COPS

I was out driving minding my own business driving down that same dirty old road. I was driving when it happened again as I was minding my own business, I past a police car. As I positioned myself over my steering wheel to get more comfortable and to get a better view, I noticed that there were no drivers, or passengers. It seemed a little weird that the police people would leave their car there. Why would the police leave their car in the middle of the country lane? I did not think for a second that there was something up. But being me I was all up for the investigation. I stopped just a few metres in front of the car leaving the engine running and the driver's door open with my keys in the ignition. Just in case there was a problem I would be able to get a quick getaway. I approached the abandoned police car. I knew straight away that there was a problem, I knew that there was something wrong, something was out of place. I shouted out to see if there was anybody around but nothing. what concerned me the most that the car was in the exact place that I found the body with the package. I looked at the car, I was scanning the car for something evidence looking at it and thinking about it. I did something stupid I touched the car I ran my hand s across the boot in that instance I had become a suspect know that my finger prints were there. I had become a suspect in another person's crime not by choice but by mistake. As I knew that I had made the mistake I shouted out, and in a few minutes I was swearing. Leaving myself open to more grief I sat down on the floor of the road thinking. I needed forgiveness I was telling myself what a fool that I had been.

As I moved my ass back to my car hoping that I could find a shimmy leather all I could find was a cloth. I picked up the rag, I walked back to the police car trying to think where were my prints as I rubbed the car boot area. Then I realised that this was a mistake also all I was doing was giving the police more evidence. Luckily after polishing what I wanted to be my finger prints off the car I realized that I had only touched the car twice. After all the confusion, I graded the cloth rapping around my hand and opened the door for some reason it was unlocked. I entered the car, I was in the car seat looking outside the window. I was not sure what to do my only thought was to break into the car to report it to call it in but I think that the police would think differently I tried anyway I picked up the CB. Hesitating thinking that the cops would come back. Mind you in all the action for the day I could have picked up the phone it would have been a lot less hassle. After calling it in I walked back to my van opening the door and getting in. throwing the clothe on to the floor while I was helplessly looking for my mobile phone I could not believe it I did not have it. I shut the door quietly as I did not want to disturb the environment about me. I was scared enough I made my way back to the police car and put my ear close to its window to see if I could hear the radio, but nothing. I walked a little bit further down the road again nothing something drew me back to the police car and now I was thinking that I should have a closer look I suppose that you could call it being nosy the thought after that was I should pull out leave things as they are. I was about fifteen minutes from my van by now including the police car. I began to feel quite worried and even more so that the officers had not returned. I was beginning to think that I just interfered with crime scene. As I looked up at the sky not realizing that I could see that far. However it seemed strange I ws watching the sky line and the sun set most of the sun was hidden behind some large clouds as I continued to watch the I could see the sun force its way through then from nowhere came a flock of birds they looked incredible and the noise I wished at that point that I had my camera with me it would of made a good picture I was looking down thinking about what I had just saw and did not catch on until I realized that they were circling may be I thought if I could found out where they were and what was there position I might find the cops. With all the excitement, I got back into my van drove off to the next village it was not too far a couple of miles. I knew where I was going as it was on my round. I was not in any rush to find them, if they were where I thought they were. Where I mapped them to be. There was no traffic which seemed weird as this road was reasonably busy. As I neared the destination I entered the small village I did not want to make too much noise as I did not want an audience so I pulled up about a hundred meters from the cloud of birds they were crazy there was loads of them. As I approached the scene carefully and hoped that I would find the missing men to the car I got into pace as I walked down the road I was thinking that this was insane. I had to question it though why would I do this it was not like me taking in to mind the last day's occurrences I should be avoiding any kind of trouble, I concluded that I was a good person and that was the end of it. it could only end up as good, but that was not to be in this case ad I was out of my depth. I wanted to turn back but part of me told me to keep going. All I wanted to see was what I was expecting it was quite clear that they had gone missing, as I presumed that what I was thinking was right. As I walked the last few meters as I looked up at the birds in the sky circling I believed that I had stumbled upon two murders. And for the second time I had found death.

CHAPTER 11
THE CIGARETTE

For next couple of days' things where running smoothly I managed to get to work on time which was something and full filled my boss's requests. As I worked more and more I could get into my work more. People where greeting me left right and centre which was helping me open a little bit more. But I knew that I had to be careful. As one to many friends could be dangerous. The more my work mates spoke about me the more welcome I felt. I was slowly beginning to fit in and have a laugh. This new attitude from my work mates was good for me. I was generally beginning having a good time, until I went outside for a lunch break I was standing with a couple of works mates not that they were friends just because they were there. On one side was the door and on the other side was the smoking area. I felt down into my pocket for my cigarettes I was surprised that my packet was empty. The postal workers looked at me like I was scum then one of my work mates was kind enough to give me one he realized my problem. I was too shy to ask anybody for a cigarette. I knew that if I just stood there someone who offer one to me. I was right a few minutes and I was offered one. I sparked it up speaking words of thanks as I inhaled and exhaled. I was grateful after I had finished I went back to work. The factory was busy and as I huffed and shuffled around the rooms.

I was slowly sorting my desk when looked down onto the floor I found a piece of paper probably left over from last week or left on the floor by the person that had took over my desk while I was getting over the boy's desk. I did not notice it before, I stopped sorting my mail and waited for a moment to pick it up as I turned around my boss was there on top of me she snapped it out of my hand quickly as quick as a gun slinger. She said nothing it was just her game, she walked off. After that I thought that it was very strange part of me wanted to know what I had just picked up and the other part of wanted to know why the boss would snap it out of my hands. The only thought was to chase her as it was my mail in accordance to the rule of the office. Eventually after a minute I pushed the thought aside and went outside to cool off. I was thinking that she was a cocky one and I wanted to confront her I wanted to speak with her. Not that I would have any luck per my work mates.

I waited patience for the next smoke it could not have been any easier again I waited knowing that someone would offer me one after that I waited for another one and got that too. And again, I got one. I had been outside for an hour. And my shift was about to end I stood there looking at my watch counting the second s before the end of the day. As my day finished it was a great relief

To finally get out of the work place and go home not that I had done any hard work. And making new acquaintances kind of helped. Keeping their relationships was not going to be easy. Every month I had been invited out into town, or to a theatre or to have a drink in some way or another I was running out of excuses. Eventually I gave in it was some guys birthday, I thought that as I was invited I should turn up even for an hour or two just to be polite. I was emailed the address and in a couple of days I had the invitation. I put the invitation in to my glove compartment. A few days past and I was looking forwards to the party. I was in my van looking for the invitation, there was a message in it it said something like do not forget to bring a bottle. so, on my way to the party I stopped off at the local offlience and brought a couple of bottles one red and two white and a hand full of beers. I got back into the van again that weird feeling was present even more so it came over e something was not right. I was thinking that I would be stupid to take it any further as I was on me to a party so I ignored it. I was in a hurry although I did not want to be the first person mind you there is no worries about starting the party. I did not want to be standing around on my own I wanted to make an entrance. As I was waiting for the invites to walk by as I was only a street away I was watching people walk by was watching the road. It was not hard spotting the partiers and just as easy watching out for the boy and girl racers. As I sat in my van watching and counting the people and cars. I was looking at the invitation, it said something like party starts at seven bring a bottle.

It was coming up to eight o'clock so I knew that I would not be the first person in there. Still I thought that I would to be too early to arrive in there so I left it for another hour. The reason why I was leaving my entrance so late was I was not too much of a partier I was quite unsociable and I had better things to do than to get drunk. I was leaning on my steering wheel with my hand s also gripped there. I wanted to get into the mood so I put on some music, radio. As I was sitting there in the van many girls walked by them were drunk, shouting and laughing as they were. They were trying to find the party. I almost recognized all then they defiantly came from the office. In a good mood, I grabbed my beer and jumped out of the van as I had no address I chose to follow them, and smuggled myself in to the party after them. it would have been easier if I just walked in, why I did not I do not know I guess that I was too shy.

CHAPTER 12
VOODOO

In any job, there is always a twist there is always someone deceiving, in fact in every job there is someone watching you even if you knew there was always one off us on the take. I had just finished my shift which was at that point was counting parcels. As I put them into my post bag, I was called away not knowing if I could leave my work station. I went anyway when I got back my bag had been moved I already knew that it was going to happen it was obvious. I could have seen it a mile away. I had to count the parcels again, after I found the bag. That would be a couple of hours more of my time. I guessed it straight away a couple of parcels were missing. Who was it though, they must have been watching me for one it was the syndicate. Being as brave as I was at that time I decided to approach them. As I finally got some guys attention I walked up to him this was Luke that I was approaching I finally got his attention he was like pretending to be busy first he was already in a conversation, he was like hold on, then as I butted in again he was like hold on, in the end I grabbed the phone out of his hand grabbing him by his shirt for a good grip, then as I held him for a few second s turned his phone off. I pushed him as I did this and started to question him. He denied it and said speak to Dave. When I found Dave, he said speak to James and so on. I was being passed around like a voodoo doll in the end I gave up. I knew from that point that there was something very wrong with the people that I had to work with. There was something wrong with the office. I guess being passed around like a dog hurts quite a bit. I was in despair I took my bag of post and left the building. The more I thought about it the angrier I got, in fact I was so upset I had to pull over. I sat in my seat and tried to understand what had just happened to me in the last hour or so. I could not believe it. As I slammed my hand s down on the steering wheel gripping tightly, another verse came up behind me he gave me a beep a long one sticking his head outside of his window, there nothing like a bit of road rage. As I pulled over in the most awkward place I jumped out of the van and walked up behind my car and gave him a mouth full I was in the mood. Not that it mattered he pulled around me and drove off. But not too far just a few meters then he pulled up. As he got out of his car I was already there on top off him just as I was going to shout at him back again my van was hit by another car. Then they got out and started screaming I walked back to my car to check out the damage. And then the driver of the car started to shout at me, more road rage. I could not believe it I did not have time to argue I just swore at him and took his details, then I went back to the first driver I just swore at him and the comment that he made me angrier for getting angry. As I got back into my van I needed to tell myself to calm down. As I did so but my methods were not working. I put the keys back into ignition and turned on the engine, I sat in the lye bay and waited a minute before finding [peace of mind and and driving into the road to continue my job. As I was still angry used a bit of speed to return me to the right frame of mind. I was really thrashing the car I was in love with driving at forty miles an hour I thought that was fast in this occasion I took it to the limit I was hitting on about eighty it was incredible I began to really in joy myself. Then I ran a light I knew straight away that I would probably be nicked or get a ticket as the area was surround by police cameras. But I did not care. Either way I knew that I would end up nicked. And two minutes later as I came around the road corner the police. I could see them clearly. I pulled the van over with two cars about me and guiled me to a safer part of the road.

The first thing that the police asked me for was a licence, I did not have one on me. Then the police asked me to get out of the car, it was usual route teen. They both stood there and asked me to get out of the car again, there approach was making me feel nervous. They started to question me I did not like it I told that I agreed that I was speeding as they took my number plate down and asked me to wait. I was just getting back into my car again I was touched on the shoulder the words were not yet my son he made me wait as he asked me to breathe in to the small plastic machine I was being breathe lazed. I could not believe it just five hours ago, I was at a party. I was not sure that if I was under the limit and as I never really drank I did not know as I tried to explain as he pushed the bottle in to through the window I was thinking that the party was a few days ago, so I should be alright. I was trying to keep the police man talking sweet taking to him then on the other hand as I was already in my car seat I could just do a runner that s means driving off. As I blew into the ventilator he took the machine to his car. He waited and I waited he returned and asked me again I said again he replied yes again then after I did he returned to his car again I waited. I was not sure of my rights at this moment I was not used to taking to the police. The gathers the rozers the fithe or any other kind of force. I blew in to the contraption again he toom the ventilator away again it took a few moments again and a last this time said I could go, however before I left he gave me a ticket it ws a speeding ticket. As I was already in the car it seemed like that I was already getting sick of climbing in and out of the van, just recently. I had a huff for some reason I pulled out and drove off, I was feeling disobedient and as soon as I past them as soon as I they had disappeared I put my foot down again but only for a few minutes or so. I was looking through the rear-view mirror I had to put my foot again only for a few minutes again. I eventually slowed down as I came to the end of the road. I was surprised that they did not make me out to be a druggy I was happy that I was under the limit at that time. Taking in to consideration that I was over the limit forty-eight hours ago, As I had some work to do as I got closer to my destination and as I approached the small village I was feeling good. I pulled up in to a car park, there was a sign saying residents only but I knew that nobody cared so we parked there any way. My attitude was now well if they can I can. It was a little bit rude to the residents however I was a post man.

As I went around doing my round as the weather persisted it was raining. I looked at up to the sky it was over cast and the clouds covered the sun from the earth. Although it looked like it was going to rain. I did not mind the rain and I often thought about it when I had spare time. I preferred the sun to the rain to be honest at this point in my life I did not really care if I got paid. I had been walking for an hour or two I was just coming to the end of the second bag, shoving the envelopes through the doors. the only threat in my job for me was meeting a dog and stay dogs they were the worst. It's like they know they hear everything it was quite funny if you could look through my eyes only knowing the experience and feeling you would know if there was a dog at the other side of the door. Most normal people would leave a beware and you would know if there was ad go on the other side e of the door. The ones that do not mostly have their mail eaten. Or never get there post I know as I have many envelopes bitten out of my hand.

CHAPTER 13
IN OR, OUT

When I got back to the office it was very quiet I could not here a word which was very unusual as it was the depot it was weird and ghostly as

I walked down towards to my place to get the next mail that I was going to deliver as I was walking I called out is there anybody there. I could sense something or somebody. Not that I minded as quiet was nice. As I continued to walk and approached my place of work. The lights went off. I called out again but nothing I started to worry and the only thought at the time was that I had come to work on my day off. That was the only solution at that time I checked and double checked my phone it was Monday. Any way as there was no here at work it gave me a chance to look around the large office. There was mostly machinery and like large converter belts. That was not a lot in my eyes. It looked a lot better when It was filled with people. I made my way up to the office. For some strange reason the door was unlocked. I walked in after polity knocking on the door after a minute I slowly pushed the office door open. And took a step inside. There was nobody in the room, so I had a little look around after I had taken position in my boss's seat. As I sat down and lent back in the boss's chair I could see where all the egotistical thought was coming from. I did not want to sit in there I was afraid that someone would walk in. even knowing that there was nobody there. After ten minutes or so I got up. And took a final look around and left. As returned myself to t5he floor realizing that it was or must be a bank holiday. As I walked down the stairs to the floor I quickly left the building. I was walking towards my car, I was hoping that I had the day off which was relevant as there was no other workers around me and no other vans parked in the car park. Although knowing that I had planned the day that I had have off not knowing what I was doing for the rest of the day as I lived on my own the only other option was to go home.

CHAPTER 13
THE JUMPER

I was on a round a couple of days later it was going to be a rough day, when I pulled up in a council estate. I knew from the beginning that something would go wrong. I was parked outside, just outside this crappy, poor, estate I was expecting danger money for this walk. Which anybody in this position would expect. I looked long and hard at the tower it went straight up into the sky it was too high it was a mind twister. I did not want to approach it I was too scared. I guess that it was bad luck or someone in the office was setting me up or even worse, may be that just the way luck rolls. Either way I was in the tower block and on my way to the top. I was having some bad feeling s about this as I was paid to do a job, I stood just outside the tower block trying to figure out if I should enter it or if I was going to dump the mail and go to the next round. As this was my first time I look for the addresses on the envelopes to the area and numbers for the block so I could get in. I pressed a couple of buttons in hope that I would be let into the tower block but nobody would answer. I waited for a few more minutes and still got the same reply, then I approached the door its self and then I realised that the door was open. I walked in it did not feel to safe just as I walk in then some old lady began to speak through the telecom she would saying who is there went on for minutes eventually it gave me the confidents to walk in so I did. As I replied that I was a post man she buzzed the door even now that it was open. I had letters all in my hand s and all to the same person and I guessed you would guess that they were all for the same person the only problem was that they wryer at the very top of the building and I mean the very top. That means that I would have to travel right to the top of the tower I did not like this, I did not want this. I would have to go straight to the top. As I walked around the block trying to figure a way out of going up the tower I could not find any reasonable excuse and in the end bumped straight into a lift it was in order I stepped inside e it funny that it does not matter who's lift you're in or however poor it may seem it always stinks of urine. I stood in there for about fifteen minutes taking me to the nearly very top. The smell got too much for me and I chose to take the stairs. But before I got to the top I had to go back all the way down stairs to the beginning I was back on the ground. I started my journey back up the old-fashioned way the stair. As stood at the bottom of the stair s I looked upward s of what I was just about to climb. At that point just as I started weather or I would make it I was deciding if I should leave my bag at the bottom or taking it up to the top way=the me, I guess that was paranoia. I tasted to make my way up to the top. When I look end in my parcel bag there was only a few letters it. the journey was a little less of worth it I really wished that I should have thrown them in the bin, guessing that they were probably bills from days ago, As I made my way slow approached it was like the air had been cut off and the heating turned up I had only been walking for a few minutes I looked in my bag I had only been up a few flights I looked in my bag for some water I did not think that I would be so unfit. I found the water bottle but it was empty there was only around about seventy flights of stairs to climb. As I neared the top that would be one hundred flights. I finally got to the top I found some air to breathe back into my lungs and mind I was knackered. But it kind of felt good. I was impressed with myself. I did not know that I could move so quickly. I posted the old lady's mail I did not know that an old person could be so noisy, some of them were quiet and other were loud some of them came to the door to greet me mostly old people looking for company in one intents I was with an old lady for an hour just taking. Some of them made me smile. Now that I had been at the top I ache=d to perceive myself down to the very bottom. My first mistake was to walk down the same way. It would have been easier if I had taken the lift. I already knew that the lift down was out of order, as I to the stairs and climb down the stairs and the lift was in order meaning that it was in service. It just caught my eyes as I passed it as I went to check it just case it was in working order. I had in bit of luck, as for now I was on my way downwards to the bottom. As I was late for my next shift I picked up the speed but as

I was moving too fast I crashed into the floor. It was just my luck; lucky I was not injured just a little sprain I had twisted my ankle. I made my way toward the lift door which was through another door and up some steps. I was hoping that it would be in order it was I was lucky and I had the smile on my face to go with it. I shut the stairs doors and limped to the lift I moved closer to the lift doors I pushed the lift door then pushed the lift button. It had the same same smell, the smell of urine it was awfull the doors on this occasion opened to my surprise on the lift floor was a body this came right out of the blue, I just stood there as the door closed I closed my eyes in disbelief jumping backwards as I met it with shock I was looking for my mobile phone. Then suddenly I heard a voice s shouting I was still on the top floor I had not gone anywhere. Well I thought I was on the top floor as I stood over the dead body I tried to contact the right authority I called out to the shouting voice. It sounded like a man that I was talking too. While I was on the phone taking, and making a report, I realized that the lift had missed my true destination and had taken me up to the top floor there was a man on the roof I was trying to put two and two together. I was outside now on the balcony what was I doing there I asked myself I guess it was in all the day's work. I began to ask the man questions probably one to many at the same time I was talking to the police, trying to explain the situation. It was oblivious that the man was going to jump and the body in the lift or there about as I was having to talk him down, reality escaped me. As I got closer to the man which I was believing that he was a killer or the person that was on the top floor I was getting closer to him within an arms distance but what could I do or even more to the point what was the strange man on the ledge doing to. There were two options I could reach out and grab him or I could let him jump.

As I stood on the ledge with the man a thousand thoughts raced through my mind I could feel my heart beating, I was thinking I was thinking that this man could not be saved. As I stood there on the ledge my only other thoughts were once that he makes the decision to jump he would jump I was thinking that his man could not be saved as I stood there with him knowing that if the man had already made up his mind to jump he would he would jump and there was no talking him down. I could hear my heart beating. And I think that if he had a stronger mind he would a step away from the edge. And I think that he should have questioned himself also if he had more faith he would have given himself the option of walking away from the edge. As I started to speak to him, I started by telling him my name. I could see that my approach was all wrong. As I started to speak to him, but his temperament was beginning to change to more I spoke the more angered he came. As I shouted back to him saying that he did not have to do what he was going to do. As more and more people began to turn up it looked to me that he had a crowd it did not help mine or his situation. As the local authorities, had finally turned up also. Now the jumper had an audience also, just as the police turned up on the roof I could get myself back inside that's when I heard the loudest cry the jumper had jumped there were loud cry's and cheers and a few wo's.

CHAPTER 14
DIRTY MONEY

It all began when I got home there was a parcel for me I had picked it up off my door step it felt quite heavy. I placed it on my small door way table, with my door keys. I was so tired from the day I went to bed, straight away. When I had awoken, it was early evening. I had left the parcel on the table to rest for some strange reason I always had the notion that you should let your mail settle before you open it, for me that was a rule I never open my mail any way. But as the day fell into the afternoon I was pressured to open the parcel I went straight to the front door and picked it up it was cool I was cool even though I did not know what was in it yet. It was quite heavy as I walked into the kitchen slowly trying to open the parcel as I walked in, it was jammed tight. Whatever was inside it must have been important, I struggled to open it by hand and went to the kitchen, in the end I grabbed some scissors from the kitchen forcing my way into the parcel through the tape. When I finished cutting through the tape I saw it, money and lots of it. I could not believe it I could not tell you how much was there it was lots and loads. It was substantial. I smiled and put the parcel down on to the table with and in shock thought who, where, why, who did this who was trying to set me up. Who sent the parcel to me? I checked the address and the label again myself. It clearly had my name on it and the seconded thing I did after opening it, I was to remove my name from the parcel. It had my name on it in big large letters. In the end, I figured it out but not until I had counted it. I was counting fifty after fifty there was so much that in the end I had gave in. It was obvious that somewhere in the office was trying to bribe me.

CHAPTER 15
PAPER WEIGHT

I laid in bed thinking about the things that had been happening the last couple of days I was reminiscing in a big way. Everything the body with the package with it. the two missing police men, my vehicle breaking down and the way people were treating me in the office. I needed more space. I could not function in my home any more I was trying real hard every time I put the problem down another one started, it that I was thin king in circles, mind you they do say that life is a circle. I do not know if I agree I heard it in some party when I was a child. I was looking around my living room I wanted to grip something with half a smile on my face but where was the rest of my smile I asked myself. Somewhere I did not know. I kind of sighed, as I was rubbing my eyes with my hand I was tried and I wanted to go to sleep, I needed a lot of sleep, although the thought was nice I decided to crash on the sofa. I fell asleep very quickly and I was enjoying the peace of it until I had awoken I was awake and still in darkness I was in pitch black there was darkness all around me. even though that I had over slept I hit my alarm clock stopping knowing that I had woke up late gain the clock said eight o'clock I was two hours late. I jumped up h got dressed knowing that I was not particularly bothered all I really wanted to do was to go back to sleep so I did as I tried to sleep and relax I found myself tossing and turning for an hour until my mind had finally decided that It would not let get to sleep again this early morning. It was the worst feeling ever the want to sleep, but knowing that you cannot and knowing that the only cure was night time. I just laid on my sofa with my hands on my mind trying to figure everything out, I could have laid there for days, I was getting nowhere fast and I was running out of time. I was basically in tears in what I had seen and been through the last couple of days. The dead body of the man, I could not get the images of the body out of my head and then there was his jump it was a long way down we were looking at least a hundred feet. The images were not going to shift it was causing a massive shift and spiritual default in my spirit and it was all on my account.

I closed my eye s once more morbid you may think the only answers were to go back to the places and try and hope that I could find answers. I already knew that I was not a detective or anything else which includes a priest or that I had known any kind of spiritual word however although now I would find myself becoming a medium, I had looked at that word I will explain it to you later. The images where moving through my mind and I had lost consciousness on more than one occasion but only for a few minutes as I could bring myself back. This happened again and again I was trying to understand what I was mint to do and what I was seeing, my mouth fell open and my eyes felt tried except I was awake I was very upset at this point I wondering when I would sleep again I closed my eyes in the last empty to find some sleep again. One hour later I was still awake. This leading to me to believe that there was something wrong. I was straight I did not want to take

drugs I was and discussing my own behaviour to myself I did not understand it. I did not need doctor. All I really needed I thought was a good night's sleep.

When I a wake but wanted to be, asleep I walked to my study and looked upon my shelves for a book although looking at so many books forced me to change my mind. Backwards then forwards as now as this was happening I started to look for a film to watch instead. In the end, I decided neither as I pushed the book that I was going to read back on to the shelf and did the same to film that I had picked out of my collection also.

In the end, I found myself a magazine it was not really the thing that I would normally do in the evening. The magazine was about year out of date. I looked father into my collection, and found some old newspapers instead. Even though I was not going to read them, I went all the way back to the beginning. I was looking down at a paper weight, as I gathered my thoughts and was trying hard to understand what had happened to me within the last six months like the way that I was feeling and this feeling had not left me. In an instant, I thought that I had been slipped something even though there was nothing wrong with my behaviour, I was not seeing anything or to that fact hearing anything. And I was normal, I stepped outside on to my veranda it was dark. It was beautiful the lake was quiet and it looked tranquil. As I looked across the lake thinking hard I still could not find the answer if there was one. Why was the feeling that I was having feeling like I was being watched? I took another step for=wards closer to the lake. As I stood there gazing over the lakes water there was no answers here. As I looked up at the moon and the stars I have had better feelings it was like I was being looked down upon but not looked after. I believe in the stars and offend discussed to myself if they were real. I knew what I was thinking and I knew I had said. As the evening went on I was trying to keep myself busy I was looking for a good article in one of the papers that I had found earlier in my study. There were so many off them again I could not make up my mind. In the end, I just pulled a large handful off the shelf and laid them in order on my desk. I was just looking at them closely scanning every word until I found some articles about politics. This was not so good it was too hard hitting I turned the pages back until I was back to the front cover. As at this point I was in two minds I was finding it exciting I pushed the paper across the table and pulled towards me off the pile another one. This was more politics I was trying to remember when I had brought the papers as I have had any account of being in politics. A small smile came across my face. as I turned the pages over this was very good I thought but I wanted something a little bit easier to understand I closed the last paper picking up my paper weight and put it down on to the page. I did not read the page as I was done with the papers for now. I went back upstairs to lay down.

CHAPTER 16
INITIAL B

I had my eyes closed and in all my thoughts finally found myself I wanted to get to walk. It was a real struggle just to get myself up out of bed. I needed a new routine before I was sucked into life of the mindless the life of the tramp. It was hitting me hard one minute I was up and the next I was in bed again it was enough to make you think like a loser. It was the same feelings every day. And that other recurring thought of parcel. As I laid on my bed I was absorbing it all in trying not to think. There was defiantly something wrong I got out of bed slamming my hand on to the alarm clock that was just force of habit it was not even on. As I went off down stairs knocking over empty beer cans from the night before. And the echo through my mind go on have another drink. I pushed the though aside it was not easy but possible. I was looking for my cars keys and found them in the fish tank. Then went to work.

It was my initial B that's what I signed in as, as I worked in the office I did not like telling my friends my real name. it was not that I was impasses it was just so. I walked in this time I got the date and time right. It was not like I was off my head like the other workers seemed to be, I was a postman.

I grabbed NY mail bag and I was getting ready to have it filled up. There was a ton of mail mostly envelopes I knew that it was going to be a long shift, there was a ton of envelopes it looked like it was going to take me all day. As I was filling my mail bag I ws slowly putting what I had to do aside and began to prepare myself for the day I left the office and was on my way.

I just put my foot down as I did something disturbed me I decided to wait I looked in the rear-view mirror, there behind there was a crowed of postal workers beginning to gather it was a smoking break. I looked again not believing what I could see it was one of my bags. I jumped out of the post van and cool but angel I think his name was Michael or something he ws turning my mail onto the floor he laughing and making obscene gestures. As I neared him he did not see me as he turned around I was there right in front of him. Grabbing what was left in the bag with the bag off him. With most of the contents on the floor I knew instantly what it was about it was the money. I had not told anybody and I now knew who was setting me up. And just so you know I was not in the mood for saying thank you. I pushed him away not saying anything and as soon as I had the space picked up the mess as the other postal workers slowly left the smoking area. If I was going to argue with some body it was going to be him and it would be today.

I jumped bag into the van looking outwards through the wind screen. It was sunny but there was also a small mist just coming off the ground I think they call it dew. Infect the more that I noticed it the thicker it became.

I drove around for a while off to find my destination but as I was driving not too far from my first port of call I had to pull over something died in my engine. I knew exactly where I was, I was pretty much in tears as I knew if I did not finish my shift on time today I would get an ear full from my boss. Even though I knew the consequences I called the office. The boss was in in the first instances as he picked up the phone on the other end I quickly put t6he phone down on mine, not thinking that he may had recorded NY number on the other end. I was now thinking that I could just see if I could fix it myself. although I was no mechanic, and I did not have the time I had only driven a mile even so it would probably cost me a small fortune for the repair and I did not carry any money with me just a few pounds in the glove compartment. I opened the bonnet to see if I could fix it. I was dreaming I did not know anything about engines as I looked under the bonnet a passer-by stopped and asked me if I needed help I had parked right in the centre of the road I said gladly yes it would be helpful. just help me push it to pavement on the other side of the road. I was talking the whole way guiding him as we both pushed the van into a small layby. I ws just inside of the van with my door open with one hand on my car door the other hand on the steering wheel. Eventually we made to the side of the road. I was lucky as there was not so much traffic. I was just pushing up the bonnet and the police pulled up. I was not happy I thought that they were going to nick me. but to my surprise they got under the bonnet with me. We stood there talking for a few minutes after they had fixed it. what was the problem he said no oil? I said thank you as they left just as they drove off leaving where they found me I got a phone call. He was asking me to come back to the office I put the phone down and headed back. There was a long pause then nothing. I was full out of excuses. I did not want to tell him about the van breaking down he would just say that's an excuse even though it was in my eyes that it was the company's fault. And I knew that he would blame me. I told him that I would be there in half an hour. I locked the vans door taking what I was going to post this morning with me again leaving the strange parcel that I had found on the road side in the van I had completely forgotten about it. how stupid was I for leaving it. when I was walking into the office I was getting some seriously funny looks as I was greeted by people that I did not even know or cared to know. I climbed the stairs to my boss's office. When I got to the door he asked me if I did not even get the chance to knock on his door. I knew straight away that I was going to be fired. I was trying to interrupt him as he was speaking, I was not able to get a word in edge ways, he was laying his law down and in the end, he said those fearful words s to anybody's ears your fired. He offered me two weeks' pay and asked me to leave the premises. I was trying to defend myself. He had an answer it was like talking a machine a washing machine or more so a dish washer. In the end, I just agreed I put the bag of parcels down on his office floor he answered that reaction like a snappy crow what was I doing he was looking at me as I was looking at him he then said finish your rounds, I left the bag where it was there was a strong silence about the both of us then I went to speak just as he went to speak. He told me that I was not out until tomorrow and I was to finish the round he claimed it was in my contract and I had no rights he did. I looked at him for a minute I left the bag on the floor and walked out. I was ready for that feeling so there was no emotion you know the kind you get when you find out that you've been dumped by your girlfriend the embarrassment and on top of that the tears, the only thing about being fired for me at least I was not in a public place. As I did not have the van I had to walk home something told me that something was still wrong it was a weird feeling like I was being watched. I still had the cars keys but know petrol I was thinking that the van did not matter as I would return it to the depo later. As I past the van on the way home I had a notion to try the van something told me that there was petrol in it I had nothing to lose so I did it revved up beautifully I drove it back down the road I was now on my way home. I tapped the sun mirror down and to my surprise there was a message the car was filled with petrol by a man and he had cleft be his number it said just call him to thank him. I put my foot down as I came of the junction, knowing that I was being watched by the road cameras that me slow down but not for long it took me about five minutes to realize what I ws doing but I knew the consequences. As I neared my home the engine began to bide in again. After that I did not look back at the guy who filled it with some petrol I was happy that he gave me enough petrol to get home. I stepped out the car looking at it like it was my wife. Not forgetting the keys closed the door for the last time. I was only a hundred feet from my house I got to my front door slipped in the keys and walked inside. After the day's events I was thinking as I sat down and took a seat. And started to sum up the equations of what I did to upset my manager and get myself fired. It could have been a few things considering that their new boy as they called it. All I could think of was that I did not play enough ball you know it was there empire not mine, I'll tell you a little secret half of the post-world was bringing it in. in saying that I had very little evidence to prove this, only the film that I made. The only other reason I could think about is that I did not work hard enough to progress, you know get in and get on with everyone that was my last theory I was out but in fact I was in deep.

CHAPTER 17
DANGEROUS GAMES

At the end of the day when I realized that I had lost my job and day set in to me that meant no more waking up early and I would have the chance sleep in if I could sleep. It also meant that I could lose my home although I enjoyed it thinking about it I could lose a substantial amount of money because of the mortgage. It was all beginning to sink in my beautiful home on the lake. As I began to sum things up I was slowly losing my mind. I was having a little mood swing and the thoughts that I was having would send you out of your mind. I was desperately trying hard to take control. As I was looking across the lake outside the large back doors the water was calm and as I just calmed down myself we were in motion I was with the element. Although now I wanted revenge. But how was I going to do it. I suppose that not returning the van was away that was on but I wanted two. I was sitting outside I could feel the cold and I could feel a cold coming on. And in an instants I could feel my nose tickling within a few minutes of that feeling my noes began to run.

I wiped the sticky mess from my nose and upper lip and then it happened I was sneezing I had caught the flu. After a few seconds of sneezing. Then I was normal again then it started again for another few moments and then I was normal again, and then quite again. I decided to quite the balcony and go back inside, it was a little bit warmer. I sat down on my seat I was just laying there staring at the celling thinking about the day's occurrences. As I sat there on my sofa I was feeling comfortable with my eyes closed I was still finding it hard to think about a new job. The only thought at the time was to be honest was and I was not that particularly clever although I just knew how to do things, in fact there was not that many jobs out there that I could probably do. In knew that and I was comfortable with that. I was looking down at my pay check as it had now arrived. It looked like I got a bit more than I expected although that was the least of my worries I was not thinking about the now I was thinking about the future, my future I closed my eyes and tried to think about my next job

at this point I was telling myself that I could do anything, this was a mistake I was getting a head of myself.
It was like a game, a dangerous game after putting down my phone after an hour making calls and searching, and writing down p [possible numbers for jobs I gave in. infect it only made me feel even worse. I ws really upset at the end of it all eventually I calmed myself down I wanted to be outside where I could shout and scream. As I looked at the lake I did not want to disturb it as it was nice and quiet, it was peaceful and I was now feeling drink and relaxed my mind fully focussed on the water, it was making me feel better and that's the reason I moved here in the first place. The area was rich and I had what I thought was good neighbours although we never spoke.
It was a lish place to be and I did not want to lose it, it was my home and it made a difference in life. I could not think about being anywhere else. A few days past and not one of the jobs that I applied for goat back to me. I was thinking again that I might have to sell up and lose my home since I had no job. Taking that thought I was paid out for the next six months it did not look likely that I would find myself another job within that time unless there was some out there who was thinking of being charitable.
I pushed my hands into face and rubbed my nose as it was itching again meaning that I would probably have the sneezes. My thoughts changed from nice to horrible to irritable I picked up the cup of coffee that I had made earlier and stared deeply in to the job page on my computer screen.

My job hunt was over for now I had, had enough, I was going nowhere for now as much as I had tried I was going to try harder. I needed to make some more phone calls I could just afford to do it as I was running seriously out of credit. In the end, I needed cash and I needed it fast then through all the thinking I thought about the parcel. I was so blind the answer was staring me straight in the face. the parcel was still sitting there in the hall way on my key table I had left it half open. I walked into the kitchen with a smile on my face I was thinking in the next few minutes I could save my life, and my home. I had found it I stood there for a few moments thinking what was in front of could be my future I was there for ages contemplating and thinking that I knew what I was going to uncover was a mint. I was savouring the moment a lot. I grabbed the parcel up quickly it was brown in colour it looked like it was from America it was large and heavy and I knew it was money, as I took the parcel to the next room away from the hall way and into my kitchen I sat at my bar and opened it up. I was in luck as the contents looked small infect it was quite large. It had money in it which mint that I was saved I had enough cash to cover myself and with that I had saved my home.

CHAPTER 18
MINT CHOC CHIP

I was in my kitchen celebrating me knew found a new occurrence there was a big bag of money and there was loads of it some of it was American and some of it was British you know red as a bullseyes and fifty's lots of them. in a way, I know it sound as a little bit ungrateful but I was wishing that these fifties were hundreds either way I had won. I placed the money out on my kitchen dinning bench I was loving it I had not yet got over the shock I was in shock I could not bring myself to count it at first. I was going to take myself outside first and enjoy the moment in fact I needed the fresh air. I ws drawing the thought father into my mind waiting for a decision and decided to wait until the evening too have a count. As I finished my cigarette on the balcony I decided to go back inside even though now I was nice and calm outside my temperament was the night in front of me. it was a nice night I stepped back inside absorbing what I had seen I had been standing there all evening only realizing that I had been outside so long by stepping in and looking at the time, I thought that up had been outside for an hour but in fact it was much longer I had been outside for three hours per my clock on the wall. When I got inside the money was still on the table waiting for me to count it. it was staring me straight in the face, I had to smile. It was time for a count.

I did not know what to do I did not really want any visitors at this moment since I did not want anybody to know that I had the money and I would only have to spread it around I could imagine the kinds of hand s out that I would have to give the neighbourhood. Just as I said that to my surprise the doorbell rang as I stepped backwards as it rang again, it must have been something important as the person on the other side of the door would not have stayed there to ring again and again. I went to the door I was looking through the sight in the door. I was still unsure about opening the door. I needed an excuse not to answer the door in the end he had rang the door so much I just gave in. I answered it with come back later then stupidly I shouted out what is your name. he answered his name it was my neighbour I told him to come back later again as I was in the bath, I had totally made that up I think he fell for it. I really began to laugh I had just received half a million it was not likely that I would just open my door top any one. And I was sure that there was no way that I was going to open me to him. I stood by the door listening to his footsteps as he walked away. He eventually left, I went outside to finished my smoke as I put the cigarettes out in to the ashtray it all in what I could see in front of me was my soul, I stepped off the balcony and walked in sideways I did not know long I had been outside. Per the clock, I had been outside for most of the day. As the night time came over and the day disappeared into the sky the smile on my face became bigger and bigger the light slowly disappeared into the night. With the money, I realized that I was finically secure I was heading for the good life. There was a knock at my door in an instant I picked up the money stuffing it into anything I could find mostly kitchen draws and pots and pans. It took me all in all about fifteen minutes I was calling out just a minute, hold on, I will be there in a minute. I ran back into the kitchen grabbing the bag which was still filled with half of the money or there about as I walked toward s the door I looked through the spy hole. He had rung the bell three or four time as I stood there by the door I was not convinced that I should answer it I walked back to the kitchen picking up the bag and softly put it down in the big cupboard I went back to then door and looked through the peep hole. It ws Darrel my neighbour news seems to travel fast.

I was walking in the high street it was about half past eight in the morning I walked right up to the banks doors I was so out of touch I did not even know the banks opening times as I stood around smoking trying to find something that I did not make me look like a bank robber. The opening times were printed so small it did not seem fair on the old. I took another packet of smoke s out of my pocket. It was a full packet I had just brought them from the shop over the road on my way. As I pulled the smoke out of its packet and lit one up. Time was moving quickly and before I knew it I was in the cue to cash and bank my pay check. It was my turn I felt a little nervous as I approached the assistant on the till. I gave her my name and address and some other details it was like everyone was watching me, what do you think that I was going to rob the bank it was that intense. Mind you that could also be the answer to my problems. Not that my problem had just been solved but there is nothing wrong with being greedy. Any way I will get to that part later we got to the point after a few second s of talking the assistant asked me how much would I want to put into the account, there was a pause on my behalf I had about five hundred g's lifting the bags saying all of this. She rang a bell as I looked around the bank as the rest of their customers began to applied. She said politely that If I could wait for the bank manager. She looked confused then sashes said how much is in there I told her that it was her job and that's why I was there. After I had the meeting with the bank manager and have him double check the count which was over the first estimate she just looked again at me there was a pause. Now my heart was racing in all my angst I just told her to hurry out as I was having a heart attack. I asked her idfnthe money was in my account after another conversation she finally agreed with the go ahead of the bank manager. I was glade that the meeting ws over I made my way home in a taxi.

On this occasion, I, did not want to speak to anybody and yes it ws the money it would surprise you how far a conversation could travel. I thought that I could keep it quiet within the next couple of weeks the whole estate knew as I was slowly beginning to live it up a bit I had brought a new car which was a little bit obvious. That I had some spare cash I ws being complemented over and over by one of my neighboured s his name was Darrel, he was basically on my door step everyday complimenting my car and having a good look around that did not surprise me half knowing him. It came to the point that he was there on my door step asking me if he could take it for a spin. I said no he persisted to the point that I would just slam the front door in his face. he was begging me but the answer was still no. then I fell father in it I had brought myself a jacuzzi the neighbours thought it was great and as it ws the summer it was time to party again it started with Darrel I invited him and he invited everybody else. Going back to the car I was so fed up in having home come to my door in the end I ended up giving in. this to me was a sign of weakness. But his persistent was a lesson. He was really impressed or seemed to be. Going back to the jacuzzi he came to my door knowing that I had only invited him but a soon as I had opened the door the rest of the neighbours followed I ws now having a house party. I had fallen in to shock even more so none of them was on my guest list. I stood there in amazement as the party went on or his party went on. As more and more people turned up all I got was greeting of hello.as they all seemed to barge past me occasionally I was handed a towel and if I was lucky a bottle of wine and a few beers summer was here.

Everybody was here and even ally I jumped into the jacuzzi tub the fun had just begun some of my guests decided to look at the shed that was sitting there beside the pool it was a sauna. Mind you that did not surprise me as it was situated right beside the hot tub. I was extremely surprised how polite my neighbours were. The coal was burning and there was now steam in the jacuzzi hut there was soft new towels in the sauna everybody seemed to be having a good time apart from me. I ws glad as inside it made me feel white the man and I ws now feeling that I ws fitting in with the local community I was feeling a little more welcome around the village. As the crowd dispersed I was happy to clean up and send the last person home, who was Darrel. I was thinking that I had such a good time I would defiantly do it again. Darrel said he would call me again even though he was a few doors away. And he said that he would call me in a couple of days to thank me for my hospitality. Although he quizzed me on his way out he had not asked me for my number it was the American way they speak funny. After a few hours of getting over the party I was tired I had cleaned most of the party mess up. I was feeling so lucky to have such nice neighbours and through that we would party again. As I looked out on to my balcony everything that I could see was on the right side of me including the sauna and the hot tub I still had the view of the lake with my garage being underground. It was cosy. I stood outside on my balcony pulling another smoke out of my jacket I lit it up the soft cessation hit my lungs. After I had finished I slowly put it out politely in the ashtray I took the ashtray to my louvre and began to sum up the day's events over all the excitement I began to chuckle. If you could see it from my point of view you would probably laugh too. It was as taste full as licking an ice cream. I was not particularly tired now however it was not normal for me to stay up. In fact, in saying that I was probably the fact that I did not have to get up at five o'clock in the morning my leg=fee was slowly changing so was my meditation.

CHAPTER 19
THE INVISIBLE

After a few months of constant partying the novity finally had worn off on my neighbour's side. As it was now winter it kind of left me feeling confused and a little bit used. What they did not know that you can use a hot tub all year round. I did it was very cool, any way I began to think that I was invisible. Not only this I missed them even though they were right on my door step. As I tried to usher the neighbourhood posy back but it was not working. So much for home improvements, they wryer not working at this point I was left alone and dreaming of the summer time. Even though it had just left. I was braking in to tears. As another month, past I was still partying. The odd bottle of wine and the occasional couple of beers. I was thinking about what I must have said to have my neighbours all of them to walk away. Maybe they wryer just users. They just hide away.
In the end in the winter at the end of the day I was happy and I had locked all the money away safely in the bank. What I did not know at the time that the money still was not actually mine. As I recall the package was sent to me by the post office per the stamp and the address. It ws sent to me without a letter, I was getting worried as I had spent a little of it. I was thinking where did it come from or who in the post office sent it to me. this is where things start getting complicated. As I no longer work for that company I wanted to approach my old boss and find out who sent me the parcel and question him over it. I ws not happy just thinking of it I was scaring myself. It was not a good positon to be in. maybe I was being framed. In the end who in the right frame of mind would sent it back. I mean who in the right frame of mind would send you half a million quid and say nothing.

In the end, I was feeling worried I was worried that some hives will be turning up, days and days went by I had become a slouch and put a couple of pounds on simply by not working. I was still nice and straight however I could not fit into some of my clothes and clothe shipping was not actually my forte. I had always lived in my post uniform I had grown out of it I did not think that I was being lazy. Any how I did not know that I was running out of time up until now. It was a curtain feeling but not exactly paranoia but close. I still had the feeling that I was being watched. I walked to the front of the house lo0cking the door shut then I e=went upstairs and checked all the windows as I went back down stairs in to my living room I closed my curtains just leaving enough room to see threw. I was slowly cracking up could feel a breeze from somewhere it was soft and it was blowing on to the back of my neck. Not knowing that it was just the wind, I closed my eyes and moved away from the windows there was nothing after that. Everything was locked up and was locked inside I was contained. In the morning, I, did not feel any different the same feeling that had changed the atmosphere of my home ws about me. I was thinking that maybe that I had a ghost. I must be crazy I told myself I did not believe in ghosts and things so I ruled it out but in my mind, it seemed real. I could just be drunk it could be to the fact that I had been partying and this was the outcome. It could have been that I was lonely. I was thinking that it could be a hundred reasons why was I feeling this way after having such a good time. I was defiantly sure that I was not going mad in fact quite the opposite. As I was looking across the kale through my curtain and sucked what was left of the night into me. it gave me a calming feeling it was cool. And with that I knew that I was going to be okay.

CHAPTER 20
ECHOES

I was going upstairs to run a shower and basically sober up something was wrong I had to ask myself what. The shower was running smoothly and I knew that when I got in it was going to be hot. Even though I was a bit reluctant to step in knowing that the first few minutes would be pain full I would normally take a shower very couple of days but dew to all the old and knew things I had been a little bit busy. I was replanting things in my head I needed a totally knew Schule since I was now that I was not working. I was still stuck in the past. It would probably have helped if I could move forwards. Of course, I had the money and I purpose that I could spend a little bit more on looking after myself. Although it did not bother me two much.

The shower was now hot I stepped in naked after a few minutes I was relax it felt quite good there was no pressure only the echoes of the past when I was a kid I had to run the bath myself my mum would never do for me. I was about eight years old and I was living on a council estate if there was no hot water I would have to strip wash my brothers who always washed before never left me any hot water, and that's why I loved this shower. My parents would only give fifteen minutes to wash. I was quite surprised that they would let me wash at all. As I was heed I was listening to the sound of the water, leaning on the tiled wall with my eyes closed, the water would rhyme every single drop would say something to me although I never had the chance to understand what the water was saying. But there defiantly a message in water.

As I stood there I was receiving all kinds of messages some were good and others were bad please do not get this mixed up with the sound of water this was totally something different. I could hear something about the money and then something else about relationships, stories of the past and stories of people here and now. Now, I did not know what I was doing or what I was stumbling upon I was slowly finding enlightenment. But however, at this moment I had no understanding of this and I had not experienced anything like this. As I got out of the shower I still had water in my eyes as I reached out for a towel which on my towel rail. As I got dried there was still soap in my eyes I dropped the towel on to the floor and rushed to turn on the sink taps for some cold water as I splashed the water onto my face removing the soap from my eyes. Bathing became a ritual I was washing every day hoping to find spiritual enlightenment. I did not know who I following or what I was getting into or what was the spiritual outcome. This behaviour went on for about a year each time I got in I would receive a knew message.

As time went on I was bathing more sand more the mo4e I laid in the water the father my mind went back. In the day, I would bathe two sometime three times a day. As I had nothing else to do. In a way, I guess that bathing was a good answer, even though that I still felt in danger it kept on going back it was extremely addictive and in the bend I was drawn back. I was beginning to over think about what I was doing and where I was sending myself even ally I sat in the bath rather than standing in the shower there seemed to be more enlightenment there. On this occasion, I, had got out of the bath there was that weird feeling again I told myself not to go back to the water I got dry and went to bed I closed my eyes believing that I would have a better day tomorrow.

As the sleep kicked in I was content with the day the only thing that I was thinking about was that it had been a year since I had a job. I was still unemployed even as I dreamed of work, all the applications and then the interviews. It all amounted to nothing. I laid on my bed half asleep wishing that I had something else to do. Apart from partying, hitting the bathroom and the tub. On top of that it was not easy getting to sleep with all the confusion. Also, knowing that the next meal would not come. I thought of gambling but as I thought about it, it was not really my style. I think that I will sleep that one off.

As I said before that it was not my way I also knew that I could do better things with my money the more I thought of money the worst I seemed to feel. I was sitting down in the living room sucking it all back and thinking that somebody had done me a real favour. In all the thinking I was thinking when will the they appear and ask me to pay their dues I could imagine that I had taken a bribe of some sort, it was only a matter of time before they start to ask me to return the compliment. The question was who. I supposed that they would try and get me on board., it was so obvious I was worried about who. In the last couple of hours, I had taken myself right back to the beginning anyone else would had left the country which was probably what they were waiting for. I was not as stupid as that or that gullible. I was thinking at this point I was being nosy and it was quite the opposite I was beginning rot lose I was losing my copiousness and on top of that my mind either way I was losing my sanity. I had to ask the question is that what money does to you. I closed my eyes lurching, looking for the want to get out.

CHAPTER 21
I HAD DYING IN MIND

In the end the bad guys always lose except that I did not think that I was one of the bad guys. In an instant, I was scoring again. After all the excitement of the last couple months, I was still trying sum everything up. You know accounting what had happened and all the excitement in the last couple of months, and what was going to happen. I was laying on my bed watching the night time sky turn to the morning. As the morning arose I had fallen back to sleep and did not awake until the next morning. I woke up early I ws in bed fighting for more sleep. It did not look like I was going to get it. I was tossing and turning. As the day grew lighter the more I wanted to sleep I cannot explain it any clearer in the end I was forced to wake up. In the instanced that I had awoke coughing and wanted a smoke or maybe I had to many smokes the evening before. I was trying to stay in bed as long as possible I was rolling on the sheets the bed duvet half over me. I could not muscle the fact that I wanted more sleep. At my age, it was impossible I was comfortable but not asleep. As I was already awake there was no need to wake up. I wanted to closed my eyes. I needed a smoke to help me into the morning the first place that I went was into the front living room I was happy but waking up was not as easy as you would seem. I was looking around the room half in there the other half of me in the bedroom. The sound of traffic blistering my mind entering my consciousness. It was the same every day.

CHAPTER 22
NO MONEY

I began to reminisce, going all the way back I not my youth I was not that old now I was around twenty-five still a young sibling in my own mind. And I was my own man. I made missions by myself. The things that I could remember were the good things like getting drunk and having arguments with my family and friends. It was not natural, at that point I had a girlfriend. This brought a present into my how and it was not liked I did not know t=what the problem was. My family did not want me to go out with this girl I found it hard to believe. We would speak every night. My evenings were under curfew at this point all I wanted to do was to stay outside so I could get on with my relationship. It did not happen. Me and my parents would, argue every evening over her I wanted more time with her but it was not to be. The arguments in the home got so intense that I had to leave my home. that was a foster home.

It upset me that I had to leave I thought that I was making the right decision it was at the time but it all went wrong. I had left my home with no money no belonging I was totally on my own. My family refused to help 0n top of that. They left me out to sink. As I was stewing down my friendships fell apart. And I was in the dark. I did not know that leaving home could cause such an upset mine for one. I was devastated although after a year or so after moving constantly around town I finally settled down for the fifth time. It upset me more that I had to leave home with no money and very few belongings what I did not know that there was no wake=liking back in.

For the last month or so I had given myself a new routine which was getting up, getting washed, then four points od=fan larger in the afternoon along with day time TV. Taking in to consideration that I was now unemployable. I was looking at it realistically. It was my fault. I could never really, he into TV as most of the programmes were for women in the morning. I could hardly think of the neighbours to invite them in to watch an episode. I was on my own, silent, I probably paid for it so I guess that I was going to have to watch it. I sat down picking up the TV remote clicking the channels first to the top then to the bottom I was having difficulty finding something to watch. I was having a laugh some of these programmes you would have to of lost your sanity to even be sitting in front of it. again, another big smile v [came pond my face. I heeded a few good hobbies I though t=t after watching that. I knew that there was golf range near me maybe I should go for a game of golf I had not played for ages. I guess it was not my style right now. I could always go swimming but again I would probably drown, I could always run that was good you get fit. I blew that out as well I was too lazy. I was trying to find a new life. If I could be loyal to myself would help a lot as I never really do the things that I think. And when I normally set myself to do something always comes up. I was always side tracked . I decided to by myself a motor bike at the time I thought it was a good idea even though I had the car. There was a little more freedom in that I thought. I was thinking that this decision was a cool one but not in the way you would think. I found a bike quickly and it arrived just a few days after I had ordered it. I was happy now all I needed was the comfordents to ride it.

I took my phone out of my pocket it was hot and sweaty as I scaled my phone down looking at some maps I lost my confidents and went back in doors. I was sitting by my window watching the machine. As I sipped a beer going through my mind telling myself how far I could have gone. Or even how much that I had the taste for it.

It was late when I had finished and I was happy to wait until the morning as I had found a route that suited me. to be honest I was not much of a sportsman. I could clearly see the vision.

CHAPTER 23
HIT ME HARD

As I tried to lay down on my sofa to rest I was accounting g the money and how much chi I had left. And how much I had spent and the money that I had lost. I had lost count when I got around to about a hundred grand I guess my countilations made sence. After all the partying and the car and motor bike. What I did not know at that point the bad guys were on my door step waiting for me. I knew this would happen already and I was prepared.

That thought sent me way way back into the opast it was not my fault and it raised the question why did the money turn up at my home. after thinking about it I knew that I was being set up. I could have gone to the police. Even though I was I was suffering of paranoia I did not want to go outside or anywhere else in that matter a fact. Even though I had spent a little bit of the money one fifth. Eventually I was thinking that someone would turn up in the end. that's what I was worried about it was not that I could not defend myself it was everything else. I clos3d my eyes again pushing the though out of my eyes and through my mind. Knowing that having no job I would probably fall poorly. As I knew through the experience before. Working kept you healthy and gave you a meaning. It gave you a place. It was normal to have a job. On the other side of that if you ever lost your way you would probably lose your mind. Another two days had past I was still getting the weird feeling a\ND on top of that I was still fearing that some heavies were on the way round to grab the stash but it was in the bank, thinking of that did not make me feel any better. I was thinking what was the most they could do not allot I thought if I did not tell them that it was banked. As my bank card s were hidden there was not a lot they could do. I knew exactly what to say. I was covering myself. As for the car and motor bike they were locked away safe. Although the hot tub and sauna might have given it away. I could just make that up it was not that I had bit ben working. I was getting a little nervous as I expected them to turn up soon in a coup [le of days or so. Then it happened I was in the kitchen clearing up. I had just had a good meal and after the knock on the door hoping that it would not be my last. Except these people do knock on doors they break them down. I jumped with suspires when I saw the man looking around my garden I did not think that he saw me. and if he did he was ignoring me. I knew straight away I took a step backwards as turned around in my kit=chin I bumped straight in to another man, Jesus I said in fright, who are you asked pretending not to know you startled me, I said. He was well built and small but looked hard with no hair. He was wearing a black jacket and a black t-shirt. The first thing I did was try and question him, I had no chance his answer to that shut your mouth where was the money. These were the words that I did not want to hear. But the words that I was scared to hear hit me. I knew this was going to happen. It was what I was worried about the last year or so.

Where was the money he persisted to ask? Inrailed I said what anybody would say I do not know what you are talking about typically sterol typed I do not thin k that he brought it. I continued that I did not know what he was talking about and prepared myself for a kicking.

As I was watching the other guy in my garden he walked towards my large patio glass doors when he got there he tried the door but it was locked before I had the chance to open it he smashed it. placing his hand through the broken glass and unlocking the door. I understood this was not a joke. He walked in. in my eyes he had broken in. I knew that this was not good and I had the feeling that it was going to get a lot worse. The first guy had got behind me as the other =one stood in front of me. I knew this as I was looking partially over my shoulder as I stepped backward s to avoid the thug in front of me only to meet the other thug behind me I had bumped straight into what was behind me with a push in the back I was back into the same position as I started with. They were going to beat me up, I knew and I did not care as I stepped backward s away from the guy in front of me I bumped straight in to the guy behind me there was a little bit odd pushing and then a big ounce in the stomach. Then they left leaving me the message return the money. I was squire surprised that they did so little as for beating me up I was supposed that they left and I was unharmed. But there was no chance that I was going to return the money I would be stupid too. After I had made a few changes to my home such as alarms systems and double locking my doors in the front and especially the back. Until I felt safe. I was thinking that the thought was should I move. As for the job as the postman I suppose the idea of two move would be a good idea, but where. It might be sensible to start over, the thought stayed with me for some time. I was really th9nking hard about what I was thinking about my whole situation. as I sat down in my chair looking around for a smoke I eventually found one in front of me it was on the floor in its packet I lit it up my thought were not my dreams as sucked it in and blew it out. As for dreams, I did not have any.

CHAPTER 24
LOOSE POCKET

It was obvious that I had my pockets lined I would not go anywhere. It felt seriously good but however it had it dangers as I was founding out. I was in the front of my house there was a garden there. When out of the blue Darrell turned up. I was mowing my lawn. And I was minding my own business as he bumped straight into me he did not have to knock. And it was like him to disturb the peace. He said hello, I did not want to speak to him let alone answer him. I was watching his approach as he walked towards me as I turned the mower in his direction he was now as close to me as you were. Putting his arm around my shoulder and stated talking. What I did not know now he had been watching me it was all about to make sense that feeling that I had it been him so he says. He told me that he had pitchers of everything. He was just about to avert expressing himself on me he told me that he knew everything. What kind of things I asked unsure of what he was going to say. He said not to question him for a cool moment.

After a long hard conversation, he told me that he had the pitchers of me I could not believe it in the living room he said. I had not done anything to rash just drinking and dancing, I asked him if he was serious. He said yes. I began to smile and played a long. Let's go for a walk he said he guide me to the bottom of the garden as we approached my pond he in covered his camera. He was blind I could see everything. The hidden camera he did not have anything on me and I was going to prove it at the most all he had was party. I knew what he was going to say next. The subject now was money. I asked him if he was going to bribe me he replied that was the ticket. As we neared the top of the garden he pulled out an envelope it had pitchers of me in the party. And he also had picture s of me counting the money. I went into so=hock this was real. I asked him how much did he want he said half.

I said to him that it was too much then I changed my mind, I had a question for him who told him to do that. He replied that it was of his own accord. I did not believe it, he ws working for somebody. He said

if I did not except his proposal he would call the law I said to him that it works both ways as in return I could tell them that he was trying to bribe me. he did not buy it. just wait I said I told him that I needed time to think. I was not interested in being jailed. I asked him to wait I needed a few days to think. I was not interested in being bribed. He knew straight away and approached me again. I was explaining that I needed time to thin k again I told him straight away one hundred thousand and that was my final offer I continued that that sum was a lot of money. I could not bring him down any father I knew that if I could not cut him down I was going to be ruined all my plans would be ruined. He walked off and the only thought was to get my own back. I needed time to think.
When I go back inside I was glad that Darrel had gone home. I was just about to burst with anger after all the things that had happened in the last few hours. It was happening slowly I ws beginning to lose and lose my temper. On top off that my mind. He did not show me any of the photographs although I was sure that he was not buffing. As he took to the bottom of the garden to remove the camera and film. I sat over my drawing room table hand son my head this was worse than having those have guys in my head I'm sure that he was lying, he did not have anything on me I was sure. I was about to cry. I could lose everything. What was I to do if he showed the pitches to the wrong people I pulled myself together I was in no rush to make a move but on this occasion a move might be the right decision.
I kind of guess that the party decided for me there was going to be no more fun. It was just the hard stuff how. I guess that was a good decision for now as I could always do it again. Thinking about where I could go left me under a lot of pressure. I wanted to stop thinking about the whole situation. I was over thinking about the position that I was in. I got so worried that I started blowing the whole thing out of proportion. As I walked in to my front room not being aware of how good it looked least at that moment I could pay myself a compliment. As I walked up stairs but only half way I forgot where I was going. As I turned away at the half way mark forgetting what I was going up stairs for. I returned myself back to the bottom of the stairs and walked into my lounge. As I sat back in my chair. The darkness that I was in was soothing all the thoughts had subsided that I had today. I was watching the lake from just over my patio doors before you came to the main balcony it had started to rain.

CHAPTER 25
PAPER WEIGHT

Later that evening I awoke it was a rough awaking, I walked down stairs half asleep. In the kitchen, I was making myself a coffee. As I closed my eyes in the kitchen I was finally realizing that I was losing my mind. I looked around for some milk and ended up finding a packet of cigarettes. I put the coffee down still hot and full. I pulled a smoke out of the packet and lit it to smoke. I sat down on my dinner bar. I was clumsy as I sat down with the cinerite still in my hand spilt the hot coffee all over myself I yelled out with pain lucky I still had some of my clothes on it could have been a lot worse. Still puffing on the cigarettes limped around in pain speaking to myself. Eventually the pain subsided and I could continue my breakfast good supper. It was not a good way to start the evening I thought. I picked up the cup and drank what was left of it then put the coffee back down on my bar. I was really thinking what I was going to do for the next couple of days it ws oblivious that I was going to have to run. But where, was the thought, I had an ante and a few cousins but there way of life was a little bit different to mine so much not my style. At this point I, did not have my past port, and I knew that it would only be matter of time when they would catch up with me. I was hunting around for an application form and I was lucky that I had found one that was easy enough I thought except it was a little bit old I filled it out hoping that they would except it. as I ws filling it in I was beginning to have my doubts. I may have just managed to escape a way out, and with that the money was mine, which was a good thing and a good thought. It mad e me smile in the end without thinking I picked up the form as I was just about to rip it in half as I was just thinking to stick it out what was the worst that could happen. But my consciousness did not let me. I placed the form on my kitchen bar. Thinking and thinking of another solution. There had to be one it was just a matter of time as there is always answer to everything I'm not saying that it will be the right answer but it would be one. There was an answer to most things. I started to think that I needed a place to hind the only place that I could think of at that time was the cellar. As it was not filled with junk it would be the perfect place to hide I had never really been down there before. It had an old door and an even older lock. Luckily the lock was in the inside. I had to look at it hard just to make sure that the door was sturdy enough to take a smashing. Even so I will take my chances even though I did not believe it was as my heart told me so. I was expecting them to visit me in a couple of days so late the next morning I found some food and a large bottle of water. and entered the large damp sombre cellar room. I was right perfect timing there was a knock on key door. Luckily for me I could stand on the cellar door way steps and just see through a crack in the door anybody who was walking in or walking out although I could not see how many of them there was since I could not see into my garden. I was right at the top off the stairs thinking that I should have made the hole in the door a little larger. I was peeking through a small crack in the door. I was looking at them I trying to think if they were the same guys that I met the other day I was not sure I did not get a good enough look. In fact, it was not them it was a postman I was deciding if I should open the door and go and greet him. I decided not too but however this gave me the chance to make a spy hole in the door. I had time. I was down stairs holding a bunch of keys I did not realise that I had so many. I was looking at the key side tracking myself I found a larger sliver key I had a large cadet beside of me and I checked if it would fit. As I playing with the keys I had to say it ws good timing as I pushed the key into the door first time the door opened, upstairs my door dell rang I waited feeling hesitant and now the door bell ringing was becoming more and more. I was getting scared somebody up there wanted a word. I opened theanine draw just as the ring stopped and the sound of my front door was smashed in. I continued to fiddle about with the opening of the cabinet and to my surprise there was not one but tree shot guns but however no bullets. As I picked one out checking it out looking in the barrel for bullets, there was none. I did not need to check the others. This should be enough to scare them away. I did not load the gun but I was hoping that its presents would make the statement. As the postman walked away as the bad guys had turned up as I remember clearly there was a bit of a fight. I was now getting nervous as they began to trash the place. By the time, they were through I had nothing left. As they left I came out of the cellar. The hiding place seemed to work and it probably saved my life. But I knew that they would be back. I was surprised that they bid not find the cellar door although next time I will have fire power.

Once I was sure that the house was clear and safe I walked up to what was left of my dining room. I did not like what I was looking at it was not my style. I could not believe that this was my home and it was in this mess they had even been upstairs I broke in to tears holding a lot of the emotion back. It ws that bad as I sat down on the broken furniture part of my living room wall fell. I was seriously un happy. I know knew that they meant business, it ws not a game that I was happy playing it was not a game that I ws interested in I was slowly beginning to realized that. I knew that they would come back eventually, even though I still refused to play ball. I had enough bottle to go outside and look around the car garage ws open and my car was also trashed. I looked around making sure that they had gone, although the van was still there untouched. I felt a little bit relived as I looked through its windows at first I did not think anything about it then I saw the package I had completely forgot about it. then I chose to disregarded it again only because I did not have my van keys with me.

CHAPTER 26
FOUR ZERO

I did not believe that I owed the money to anybody as it was posted to me and it had my name on it. going back to how I manged to get my house smashed in. I knew what was coming next. My neighbour and it seemed to me that he told everybody who I mixed with last summer to antsy clear of me through the grape vine. He was telling people that I lost it that I was completely crazy. I need time to think about this as the neighbourhood was just about to throw me out. I needed to get into his mind if that was possible. How was I going to do this after all he seemed to think that he was polite and he also seemed to think that he got on better with his neighbours than me. either way I did not like his snootiness, he ws the worse as he was probably bribing them like he was trying to bride me. just as I closed my eyes to think my doorbell rang. I did not want to answer it since my gaff had been trampled on. T6he doorbell rang again in the end still welding the shot gun I went to the door the postman had come back I stood behind the door slowly opening it to the point that it was ajar. I asked who ws there he handed me a letter and said that he meant to deliver it this afternoon but he said that he was forced away he then replied if I was all right. I opened the door and looked at him. I could see Darrel in the back ground was this another joke I thought. I chose not to think about him I took the letter said thanks. I was not thinking about the letter I was thinking about Darrel, I will not tell you how I really felt about him. I pushed the postman out of the way while we were still in conversation I did not walk up to him but I ran up to him. He was just getting into his car, he was belting up and just turning his key in the ignition. I could see that he did not want to talk to me, my hands were on his bonnet both I was clearly angel as I moved around to the driver's side of the door to shout at him he could of ran me over and I was lucky afar all my shouting that I got away unscarred I yelled once more at him as he drove off. The post man just stood there looking on in amazement. I walked up to him and asked him in a polite manor if there was any more mail for me he asked me to hold on as he check his mail bag. He put his down trying not to look at me. I knew why, he then pulled his hand out of his bag and said no, no as he flicked his hands through the post. While I was there I asked him for Darrell's mail. He replied that it ws against the law to interfere with anybody else's mail it was accounted as feud. I was so angry and I knew that he had a hand on Darrel's mail I polity said what is that over his shoulder as he turned away I grabbed the mail which was Darrell's out of his hand then ran back inside doors slamming and locking the door behind me. there was loads of it, I guess that Darrel ws I a little bit popular or even more per the first letter in debt. The post man was a little bit disheartened thanks I said cockily as he ws on my door step trying to defend himself he was asking me not to take the mail he shouted out threw my letter box that he could get the sack. He continued that he could lose his job. We stood there face to face I told him no one must no. then I told him that he should just agree and shaved him away. I knew that taking my neighbours mail was closure but opening it was against the law. I put him right I told him just agree and explained that I was a postman also. He finally gave in and walked back to his van. My place was still in a mess and it was going to cost me a small fortune to fix it. I could see in the end that I would probably be finically secure if I just sold although I had hoes insurance I just wanted to get out. I [laced all the mail on top of what ws left on my dining table. I was no longer thinking about the money. I was now thinking what was in my neiboures mail. I also knew trhat if I ws to open any of it I would be against the law Freud I sat there and told myself the score it was four nil.

CHAPTER 27
BE A MAN

It was late and hot and I had just finished tidying the mess that was left from this afternoon the rooms in the house. There was only one thing after I had thrown all the damaged parts out it was that there ws a big hole in my living room wall. This was not good as it was situated just beside the patio doors, having g a lake next to me forced the small elements of the country side to suck the warmth out and the cold in. I knew exactly what to do I thought I would just grab some clothe and use some masking tape and bobs your uncle hole in the wall fixed, may be a couple of bed sheets would do the trick. By the time that I had finished taping up my wall it was midnight in fact it was early hours off the n=morning. Although as the masked wall was all that I could see but it was working.

Again, I knew what they would come back within a couple of days I was laying low due to Darrel and I bet that he if he was approached would send them to me. I hid in the same place shot gun to the ready. If he was trying to frill me, it was making me feel a little hard. I feared most things and but this time I had a chance a chance to make myself a man. I ws just sitting there in my chair well what was left of it. infect I had been waiting so long it drove the madness back to me. every couple of minutes I just wanted to get it over and done with. I could not help but think that there was always while I thought about it t=someone was going to enter my door with all the damage it was left broken and I did not realise that up until now after I had double checked it. I was fed up with waiting so I went upstairs a then back down stairs all the locks were broken.

As evening became night and night became morning again nothing I could not hear a sound nothing from the lake nothing not even a bird. I may have paid my dues. I was thinking that if they had not come back now ten I had won they would not come back at all. Maybe they had given in. mind you five hundred thousand was a lot to forget about. After I sat there and finished summing it all up the cons and the pros I did not say a thing. I knew that they were still there they were just waiting for me to make the mistake. I did not know all I knew is that I did not make many bad missions in saying that to myself it kind of made me feel better. I wanted a cigarette it would make me fell even calmer. As I smoke d the smoke it was like time as the smoke s disappears life does too.

If that makes sense but the smoke never runs out and I could easily have another. It was early but dark I was surprised to see that many people so early in the day I was standing by the front door thinking about how I could fix the lock before I had to call the locksmith. They were kale robots all getting in to their car at the same time with their good days as they said good byes their wives at their doors. To me it was strange I had never seen that before there was something defiantly new and weird about the neiboourhood.

I was being a man and blowing the whole thing out the while thing was an upset. I was thinking it just did not seem right. The people going back where just a little too nice. And now that I knew about Darrel it made me sweat intensively I was still looking outside and the people kept on coming. In the end, I went to my door but something happened as I opened it and looked out of it the people were gone there was nobody. I asked myself again was I losing my mind. I looked around at first then a bit farther down the street nothing when I got back in after a good look around I was thinking that someone was playing around the thought stayed with me all day long. I knew straight away that it was Darrel he had bribed the village to do that and awful trick but how ws I going to get him back on top of everything else. I walked to my balcony then on to hard wood veranda looking over my lake. I was thinking as it started to rain the only worst=ds that I could think about was I would give you double.

I stepped back inside drying off what little rain had fallen upon with a fresh towel I was reasonably upset. Once I was dry I was thinking about Darrel again I was already upset from the day that I had met him. I thought he was a friend n=but in fact the opposite. The total opposite I need to be aggrieves I needed a punch=h bags all I could do now was shout it did not make much difference. My temper was now getting the better of me I was try my hardest not to shout. I was in control just. I did not need pray although there was not anybody around me so I had nowhere to channel the anger. I had had this experience before when I lost my job I closed my eyes. I began to control the thoughts away I cannot remember how I was taught this but it was so. I was finally calming down after an hour I was as cool as a bunny rabbit. I was enraged again I ws beginning to think t5hat this whole day ws not like me.

With everything that had happened in the last few hours I really deserved a break, with the money that I had left over and if I was to totally disappear it would raise suspicion. I decide again to stay put pushing the thought of it to the limit with that thought I went to bed. In the morning, I woke early am and made my breakfast.

CHAPTER 28
CREDIT CARD

Late in the morning I arose I decided to find out what the year's damage was that would be in modern terms how much money I had spent. I ws not really in a suitable place as I placed my credit card in to the machine heaven knows I just should have walked in to the bank that I was standing before. The problem then was it was right in the high street and it felt like everybody was watching. I got the statement and I did not have time to look at it due to the paranoia. I got back in to my van fast forgetting that it was no longer my van and I should have returned it to the office. It could be a crime offence as I no longer worked for the company. However how I got in and out of town fast I did not know why I was so scared and I was surprised that the engine lasted. I had got and out with a couple of thousand I was heading home feeling rather pleased and when I looked t=at the receipt I was extremely flush. As a coup [le of days past I was expecting Darrel to approach me for his share but there was none. Darrell knew something and he was being pushy. He wanted a hand out and was trying again. Somebody had tipped him off or maybe I was being careless. I had not mentioned in any of our conversations the word money or anything else. And was slowly beginning to think that it ws me. I was beginning to think that I got to flash too quickly. Darrel did not know anything about me he was buffing he was playing a very dangerous game and it was with me. I sat done in my living room all he had on mere =e was a couple of parties. And that's was it. although it was interesting he=why he was trying to bribe me. maybe he ws money greedy a money grabber, maybe he thought he and believed that I was vulnerable I did not know. However, it was obvious why he was trying to bribe me, it was obvious that I had spent too much money. I ws in the kitchen at the time of the call it was Darrel's turn now. There was a knock at the door I had hung up before I had picked it up I knar=we it was him as I walked through my loge and the=rough my corridor switching off the lights as I went through to answer the door. I knew that he knew and wanted a cut, it was not going to happen. I guess the sauna and the jacuzzi ws a giveaway. Even so I was right it was him he was standing at my front door realising that ivy=t was unlocked he entered it he was in my corridor as I was just walking into it. I ws hoping that he would not turn up but he was real he was sin my home. he was there giving me the big one he had started. He ws telling me the low down if I did not give him the money and why and other things like he would call the police and other thing like he would so he was claiming that he had me NY the bollocks in fact it was the other way around I just did not have time to think about it. I did not want to hear this right now there was other things on my mind like the real owners of the money. I was not going to say anything else, and I did not want to hear it I was trying to show him the door as he spoke to me I slowly got him close enough to throw him out telling him to try again later I was sup pride that I even said that. He was going on about a settlement. The argument went on for another hour on my doorstep. He pressured me so much I had to grab him which was not like me and on top of that he shouted that's grievers body harm I told him to hop it. and I told him he had nothing on me. I made that clear as I rammed the door shut wedging some paper in the door so least it was secularly shut for now. But the b=next day he came back and the arguments continued, first the photographs, he really believed that he had something. he saying and kept on saying he had something he had one on me. that was a lye it was so oblivious if he was going to the law he would have had done that by now, I was not buying it. slamming down the evidence on my table he said I could keep those as he had more. Then he continued and on. I wanted to punch him in the face but violence never solved the problem. In the end, I asked him to leave he refused ashes said we should talk about it some more I got angry and pushed up to my front door. I was unhappy and getting angrier as I was in his presents. I was not just angry that he approached me but I was angrier that he was trying to thimble as deal that would never happen. In the end, I just said yes just to get him out of my home. the next day he came back I was smoking a cigarette and I was drinking a beer I did not know why I ws being so polite to him, I just wanted to throw him in a ditch. But going back in to his world I was not happy about him be=netting mine. He came around again this time he did not even knock I defiantly needed a lock smith. The nearest lock smith was an hour away and he was fully booked per him and said it would take a couple more days in agreed and hung up. As for my neighbour, all I wanted him to leave me alone he was on my doorstep like my old girlfriend. In all of this I was feeling vulnerable on this occasion I did not go to the door to listen to his mouth and his stup[id ideas and offers. I did not want to listen to a con artist and that's what I think he was. And if I should know better he was trying to go to work on me. I should have told him where to go and I had to agree he was a little bit assistant. In the end, he was on my door every day for a month I had, had enough I had lost my temper with him. This time I a going to approach him instead of him approaching me. he was going to learn the hard way. It was two o'clock in the morning I started off to his car he should have kept in a garage I smashed it up completely the neighbours came out all of them. I walked back to my house there was a crowd of people but I knew as soon as it calms down then the next morning I would hit him again. This time I walked outside planning to remove his cars wheels and I did nobody knew even though the neighbours knew they were to whimpers to tell. I removed his wheels and left his car on bricks. There could be a lot things that I could do to him including a smack in the face but I thought that was enough for now. The next morning, he was at my door back in his world I was not happy about entering mine he came around again this time knocking on my door polity. I knew that it was him, all I wanted was for this guy to leave me alone. In all this his visits left me feeling in danger. On this occasion, I, did not answer the door. I ws not going to let him in I was not listening to this man. I did not want to listen to his offers or bribes and I defiantly did not want his relationship. I was busy telling him where to go. A couple of days later he was on my door again this time I was going to approach him again I was thinking that I was going to do more than beat up his car. It Ws one am I knew that he made it early payback time for smashing up his verse.

As he knocked on the door I casually walked to the front door and opened it, he believed that I was going to let him in but instead but infect it was going to be the other way around. As he tried to push past me I stopped him somehow pushing him back out of the door way giving me the room to raise the bat. I pushed him side and t=raised the bat. Back in his world I was not happy about him entering mine. This time he knocked on my door around the back, I knew that it ws him.

All I wanted was for him to leave me alone. He was quite clever as he was trying to tell me that we needed to talk he was persistent as now he was knocking on my patio doors and saying h=that we needed to talk. I refused to let him in. As I was calm at this moment it could have been a lot worse as I could have a bad temper also. In the end, he returned himself back to the front of the house, as he tried to force the front door just as he was going to break through it I opened it fast and shut it extremely hard into his face, I heard the screams and with it cries of pain you've blinded me you he continued to yell I think he was just yelling to draw more attention to himself and bring the neighbours out. He was not finished yet a few minutes later he was around the back again when I saw him again. I was slowly getting upset. This time I went outside to join him but instead of greeting him polarity I grabbed him his collar and then took him by his ear. As I dragged him around to the front of the house pushing him on to the floor. Something was said and I went vocally ballistic on him. I had hit him so hard verbally he got up and left but I was sure that he would come back it was just a matter of time.

CHAPTER 29
THE HARD FORK

As I sat down on my chair I knew that I was driving myself into madness, I had drunk so much on my own. I was beginning to lose touch with reality. All the village spoke about day in and day out was my money. I could guess who was speeding the word. It was Darrel I could not think about anybody else I could not stop thinking about what he was thinking, it was a curse I was sure. I sat backwards improving my position and view. I was looking for another drink I was on the brink now of saying that I really did not care. I wanted him to leave, I wanted him to die. It was six o'clock in the evening I was smashed that's drunk. I was about to start entertaining a few demons. My darkest thoughts had arrested me. I stood up then sat down opening another beer and knocking it straight back. I woke up in the morning still hung over then fell back to sleep again. It was a little bit rough I did not enjoy it. All in all, I began to feel sorrow I wanted a better way to escape. As I sat there in my chair all I wanted was another smoke. But I was so drunk I could not get out of the chair. I did not move and inch. I was telling myself to get up and in the end ended up on my floor in a slump on one side getting up was not going to be easy or waking up for even that matter. My brain was telling me to awake but body would not full fill it. I did not think that there was anything s] else wrong I was just drunk.

In the end, Darrell found me and woke me I burst into anger as soon as I saw him I was shouting at name and asking him how did he get in he said the front door was open. I threw him out with a large swearing word. And that is as much as I could remember. I continued to get drunk I know that you understand it was my way to escape the things that had occurred after having my home smashed in and losing most of my possessions, and then finding out that your neighbour was a freed. I think in those circumstances I had the right to get a little bit drunk and have a little bit fun. I sat down with my eyes closed trying to visualize a better place, but nothing. What was in my eyes were not my future but probably the past I was trying so hard to find another way and understand. But this time there was no understanding. I moved to the kitchen area which was still damaged, as I picked up one of the bar stools and sat on it I ws thinking that it had been kind of cool all the excitement, arguments and party's. I would always take my problems to my bar it was a cool place to be. It was a place where I could be it was also a good place to argue except on this occasion I was the only one there. In the end the fork meant nothing it was materialistic. Although as I was on my own it gave me a little bit of a chance to focus and keep myself thinking. As those kind of thoughts were keeping me alive. at the end of that day it was not the fork doing the speaking it was me. the fork did not speak to me neither did it smile it just sat there. In fact, I did not know if it ws eve real. Or what I was going to do with it. or what was it supposed to resemble. What I wanted from the fork was a conversation. But it refused to speak to me why I asked I presumed that the fork could not talk. And it was now giving automations. I stood up leaning on what ws left of the bar as I was leaning over the fork, told the fork to speak it did not I continued to question it I when I had finished I went back to my living room after telling the fork not to move. At the end of the day I guess that I just needed someone to talk to and talking to the fork was just a bit of fun. At that point I realized how lonely I was. Now being lonely had stuck into my mind, I was answering my own questions things like what am I doing here as like why I hanging around at home. and another thought on the similar lines. After I had been sitting there for a couple of hours it just seemed so real closed my eyes.

CHAPTER 30
SEEING THE LIGHT

I was thinking about the money and I was thinking that I should be living somewhere else somewhere like abroad it was not like I did not have the money, somewhere super rich, or even India.
I could easterly move there I would have servants and cooks and all the nice things. Even more so the woman. That's where it stopped I as dreaming I shoved my bedding aside thinking how did I get into my bed I just did not remember but I was there. I closed my eyes hoping to fall back to sleep to find that dream but I woke up instead. As I got up off my bed I felt dizzy and went straight to the toilet I undid my shorts and turned on the hot tap. I was not sick I was just waking up. As I finished using the toilet I felt a little hung over. I turned off the bathroom lights walking out closing the door behind me. I did not seem right although there was nothing wrong I was busy okaying me myself if I was feeling ill I would have told myself that. I shrugged it of to be a hangover. I was too busy any way to be poorly so I continued to think what I could do for the rest of the day. I returned to my bed room. Although at this point I did not want to be in there as it did not feel right. I was feeling a little unaware and out of place so I went down stairs again. I got on to my sofa to think but with all the thoughts fell asleep. It ws not taint was lazy it was that I had to reschedule my day. And reteach myself to do things with my time. Somehow in the period of five minutes my life was going to change for the better. I got a phone call from my old boss. Yes, the post office he was speaking to me trying to make the whole conversation exciting and I guessed was as he had offered me my old job back. The feeling in my soul was of delight. I sat down after pacing around my living room. I could not believe that it was true. And I continued and asked him if he was joking. He replied "no". he said I was to meet him in the office later in the week and said that I could have my job back. I was

jumping with joy I was really pleased. I had still had the van it was parked locally, I was employed.

I sat down after all the excitement I had won. It felt like a million bucks it ws like finding gold I a gold hunt. I closed my eyes I knew that I had made it again. I was extremely happy everything was going to work again. In clouding the party's. I got back to the depo I ws greeted with lots of cheers. Although I had got my job back I still did not trust anybody. since they sold me out the first time. Once I was in the office I found a seat I closed my eyes together my thoughts it was like I was in a totally new place. I was not stupid I still believe that there was something was wrong.

As I got into the van I was happy with the morning days' outcome. Thinking that I could get back to work but I was wrong there was no fuel as I pushed the keys in the ignition and turning the engine on there was fuel well I thought there ws no fuel as I gave it one more twist of the key the van started. I was on my way however I did not know how far the van would go. I did not notice at first but there was a storm brewing, but not just any storm with in around fifteen minutes the weather changed dramatically one moment it was sunny the next thunder and lightning. And within a few minutes after that it began to snow. It also became dark. The snow came down very fast and in the end I had to pull over, I had to call in sick not a good idea as it was my first day back. I turned the van around and headed back home. when I got back I parked the car next to my car outside my home. I was a little upset and just wanted to close my eyes. I did not want to fall asleep in the van but I just had to close my eyes for a minute but however I feel a sleep totally not the knowing outcome.

I was asleep so I did not know or have any recollection of what or how the next thing that happened. I think that I woke up through the van being so cold. I was half asleep when the shock of being woken had left me I was checking my surrounding as the wind screen was covered by snow mostly ice. How long I had been there I did not know what I did know was I was trapped inside. As I tried each door I found that I was totally blocked in.

As I continued to struggle with the door every five minutes it would not move. I eventually gave in. there was so much snow about the

Verlie I realised that I ws trapped in. I tried my phone and got no signal. It was getting colder but I knew not to panic. As I sat in the drivers chair there was silent as I was trying to figure w] away out. Then the package in my back seat caught my eye it had taken my attention from getting out to what the hell is that ticking in the background. This was the package that was in the dead boy's hands. As for being stuck in my seat I could not reach it. due to not having the room in the car to manuver. At this point I just left it again but the ticking was playing on my mind. The package was now on my mind as I slowly reached out for it again I could just reach it to touch it with my fingertips. I waited a few minutes again this stretching as far as I could reach, I was not getting anywhere fast. I was going to give myself one last go as I tried again I just about manged to reach its sides I was pulling slowly towards myself but then it happened not for the good but for the worst I knocked down between the seats I think it went behind the driver's seat.

After about half another the package was on my mind again the constants ticking. As I started to think about the body and how I had found it, I did not think that it was ticking when I had found it and I was thinking that it had just started. Exempting to reach the pagane slowly wiped the smile off my face as there ws no way that I could reach it now I ws beginning to get nervous there was no way that I could reach the parcel from inside and on top of that I ws snowed in and could not leave the verse. The van was too small to get around it. it was a small van. It was too small. As I tried for it once more I found myself stuck trapped between the front and back seats. While was trapped in between the two seats in fact it had made it easier for me to make just one more attempt I was closer to then before. I reached around bending my arms and twisted my hands. I just about managed to reach it. I congratulated myself but only for a few seconds. I put the parcel done in the passenger seat. That when I heard something I thought it was the dash board. It was so quiet you would just about be able to hear it with human ears it was not the dash board it was not that I may have had my indicators on it was the parcel. I picked it up it was light weight, I put it to my ear it was defiantly ticking in that moment it hit me the scariest thought, I thought it sounded like a bomb. I spoke the words there was something like it could not be but it was, and then again. I did not want to open the parcel it could be a clock and I wanted it to be. I said it over and over to myself. I wanted to get out of the van none of the four doors that I had next to me would shift. I then tried to kick the window screen through but I had no luck, and t's when the ticket got louder. I shouted out being scared of course but nobody could hear me. I had just lost my mind. Then out of the blue I could hear a tapping noise a knocking there was somebody outside of the van I shouted again help I'm in hear as I recall. The knocking cony=tied for a minute or two more. I was shouting that in her that there was somebody there.

Then there ws silence again then an hour later it happened again some body was approaching the verse but this time I could hear a different noise I was being shovelled out. I had a big smile on my face and was finally feeling a lot calmer. As the snow was slowly being taken away so that I could see the daylight I was felling safe again. However, time was running out the package was still ticking. As more and more snow was being removed an hour later I could see through the car s wind screen I was just at ease. As I looked through the window there was the black women the old lady the lady that I was having round for tea. A is finally got out of the car I dragged her down the road wanting to get as far away from the verse as possible. The road was Icey and filed with snow and I was yelling that there ws a bomb in the car. As I sat doe-win to rest on a snow bank I was thanking her for my life. She asked me what had happened I thought that I should n]be asking the questions. She asked me how I got into that situation I told her in the most extraordinary way as I became a bombing mess through the shock I told her that there was a bomb in the car. I continued for about five minutes and we should go back inside to discuss it over a cup of tea.

After we had discussed it and it made sense she asked me if she could see the package I said to her as if she was crazy no, but she insisted I could not stop her I tried to tell her over and over and in the end bowed down to her I gave her a warning she might not like what she was looking at. I tried to tell the old lady again as she walked out to my car park I ws watching her I shouted to her be care full. I do not think that she was listening. I told her that it was ticking and then hid by the side od =f my other car. She thanked me as she came out of the van she was walking towards me with the package she called it her passenger. When ewe both got inside she placed it on my table in my kitchen she looked at me in a strange way. Because the bomb was not a bomb, it was the old lady's clock and it had been stolen from her trolley.